THE BURNING OF NJAL

Other books by Henry Treece published by the
Children's Book Department of The
Bodley Head

LEGIONS OF THE EAGLE
HOUNDS OF THE KING
THE CHILDREN'S CRUSADE
MAN WITH A SWORD
THE EAGLES HAVE FLOWN
VIKING'S DAWN
THE ROAD TO MIKLAGARD
VIKING'S SUNSET

HENRY TREECE

The Burning
of Njal

Drawings by
BERNARD BLATCH

THE BODLEY HEAD
LONDON SYDNEY
TORONTO

© the Estate of Henry Treece 1964
Illustrations © The Bodley Head Ltd 1964
ISBN 0 370 01060 4
Printed in Great Britain for
The Bodley Head Ltd
9 Bow Street, London WC2E 7AL
by Unwin Brothers Ltd, Woking
Set in Monotype Ehrhardt
First published 1964
This edition 1972

Contents

CONTENTS

Introduction to Njal's Saga

ABOUT the year AD 867 the dark duck-shaped volcanic island called Iceland was discovered by a Norwegian sea-rover, Naddodd, when his longship got blown off-course and missed the Faroes. Iceland lies just outside the Arctic Circle and in Naddodd's time its climate was kinder than it is today. Nevertheless, the main crop to grow on its thin soil was hay and the 60,000 Northmen who finally settled on its 40,000 square miles of rock were forced to become farmers and fishermen in order to survive.

In most essentials there has been little change over the centuries. Even today less than a quarter of Iceland is habitable, and of this quarter the greater part, by far, is grazing ground: three-quarters of this grazing is given over to sheep, and the rest to cattle, horses, pigs, goats and poultry. One-third of Iceland's total population is occupied in agriculture and a quarter in fishing. Mutton and dried fish are the staple foods and there is no fruit grown, except rhubarb and, in the late summer, bilberries. Two Icelandic delicacies are Hákarl, which is half-rotten shark, and sheep's udders pickled in sour milk.

Throughout its history, visiting voyagers have spoken harsh words of Iceland. A tenth-century poet called it 'a gallows of slush'; Hakluyt declared that one could find nothing but stockfish there; and even the Viking, Ketil Flatnose, prayed fervently, 'To that place of fish may I never come in my old age!'

Other writers have commented on the poverty of the islanders, on their ugly-shaped mouths, their pale pebble-like eyes, their flaxen or carroty hair, the fierce frowning of the girls, and the general lack of interest in the world outside Iceland itself.

This sullen independence is Iceland's oldest quality. The first settlers there were heathen Norwegians, Danes, and seafarers from the Norse colonies in Ireland or the Hebrides, who were weary of the laws of their homeland, and who banded together to form a commonwealth with its own parliament, or Althing, and its own code of laws. The men of this republic admitted no kings, but instead had thirty-nine farmer-chieftains, who also acted as priests and made offerings mainly to Thor. Christianity came to Iceland fairly peacefully in the year 1000, though over a hundred years earlier one of the chieftains, Thin Helgi, who was half-Irish (probably like Njal himself), called himself a Christian, named his farm Kristness—but always prayed to Thor 'for sea-journeys and in times of crisis'.

This stubborn waywardness can be seen also in the Icelandic code of laws, which were administered for two weeks each year, in late June, by the Althing, on the plains of assembly at Thingvellir. During these assemblies the chieftains tried cases brought before them by the freeholding farmers, who formed the basis of the Icelandic community. However, though judgement was given, the independent farmers would not always accept it as final and often took to sword or axe to settle their grievances privately.

Out of such quarrels, feuds often flared up among the families and rough vengeance led on to further ambushes, further law-suits, further feuds and so bloodshed, in a never-ending succession.

8

Icelanders were hard northern folk, who lived in hard northern weather, on hard northern food, against a hard northern landscape. To expect from them the delicacy, the subtlety, the colour of Persia or Constantinople, would be a forlorn and almost improper hope. Or, to put it another way: the men and women who were quite suddenly drawn or flung northward towards this island near the Arctic Circle after AD 867 were, in all essentials, various remnants of the same Nordic or Aryan stocks which had tormented Italy, Spain, and North Africa for half a millennium. In truth, there was nothing to distinguish them racially from the Gauls who sacked Rome in 390 BC, the Goths who did the same in AD 410, or the Celts of Vercingetorix who pushed Julius Caesar so close to defeat in 52 BC. Iceland, indeed, was the last migration-place of the northern folk: it was their final refuge, against whose volcanic rifts and rocks, mountains and rivers, this fair-skinned people who had set forth as Steppeland cattlemen before the time of Homer, worked off their furious energies against one another, and no longer against great Mediterranean empires.

As Njal the Wise of this story said, 'With laws shall our land be built up, but with lawlessness laid waste.' By the year 1262, the feuding farmer-chiefs of Iceland had so weakened themselves, so drained their republic of its virile blood, that the King of Norway took charge of them and made them his subjects as though they were irresponsible children.

From this true story of Njal's burning, first written down by an unnamed Icelandic author around the year 1280, we can learn much about Northmen of the tenth and eleventh centuries: the constant bickering among farming families; the arrogant pride of men and the bitter taunting of women;

the ruthless following of useless feuds; the almost casual
manslaughters in ambush; the carefree piratical voyaging
abroad; the fearful belief in dreams and omens. Among
these people, unthinking action is followed by paralysing
remorse; tenderness towards children by such savagery as
is expressed in the horse fight; the insistent asking of advice
by bullying and wry murderous jesting. After the long and
silent holding of hatred comes the sudden snapping of
patience, set off by the tittle-tattle of gossiping beggar-
women. After a vengeful hunting halfway round the world,
comes the dying down of all anger and the making of
exhausted peace, as though the fury of the Icelandic storm
had blown itself out.

In the whole of mediaeval European literature before
Cervantes and Shakespeare there is no other story to equal
Njal's Saga for its minutely-observed and earthy des-
cription of day-to-day life in a peasant and warrior
community. Monkish chroniclers in other lands were concerned with kings and great battles, with high statecraft
and religion: but the unknown writer of *Njal's Saga* is
talking to us of farming and seafaring men who, though they
voyaged away laughing among kings and emperors from
Dublin to Constantinople, were always more concerned
with their hay-harvest, their corn-sowing and their farm-
building than with foreign titles or empty honours. To them,
their local good name, the welfare of their families, the state
of their steadings meant everything and, to protect these,
they would go to almost any extreme of trickery and even
violence.

In its strangely twilit and doom-driven way the Iceland of
Njal's Saga, with its threatening dreams and its sudden
screaming ambushes and crackling flames, is as familiar to

us as a grim fairy-tale, half-heard in early childhood; it is about the lives and deaths of people very much like our own ancestors; and, though nowadays we may know of other, more proper ways in which their problems might have been settled, we cannot help feeling a strange sympathy with thoughtful old Njal, scornful Skarp-Hedin, ruthless, faithful Kari, and even vinegar-tongued Hallgerd—that tall blonde-haired beauty, who strolled with her maidens at the Althing, dressed in scarlet and lace, to captivate the fierce sea-rover Gunnar with one bold glance of her ice-blue eyes.

The Important Dates in this Story

———

AD

874   Iceland first settled.

930   Njal born. The Icelandic Commonwealth and Althing created.

940   Hallgerd born.

945   Gunnar born.

970   Gunnar regains Unn's dowry.

974   Gunnar marries Hallgerd.

983   Hallgerd steals from Otkel.

985   Otkel rides Gunnar down, and is killed by Gunnar at
Rang River. In this year is Hoskuld (to become
Hvitaness-Priest) born.

986   Gunnar ambushed at Knafahills.

989   Gunnar kills Thorgeir, son of Otkel, and is banished.
Helgi and Grim (Njal's sons) and Thrain (son of Sig-
fus) go abroad.

990   Gunnar killed in his steading at Hlidarend.

992   Thrain returns to Iceland with Hrapp the Mischief-
maker.

994   Njal's sons return with Kari of Orkney.

995   Thrain Sigfusson is killed by Skarp-Hedin.

1000   Iceland converted to Christianity.

1005   The Fifth Court established. In this year Hoskuld,
Hvitaness-Priest, marries Hildigunn.

1009   Mord the Liar begins his backbiting.

1011   Hoskuld, Hvitaness-Priest, murdered in his cornfield.

13

1011 The suit at the Althing comes to nothing. Njal's family and steading are burned by Flosi and his band.

1012 The suit for the Burning and the Battle at the Althing. Kari and Thorgeir seek revenge on Flosi.

1013 Flosi and the Burners sail abroad. Kari follows and kills Gunnar Lambason in Orkney.

1014 Kari slays Kol in Wales, and Flosi goes to Rome.

1016 Flosi returns to Iceland.

1016 or
1017 Kari is reconciled with Flosi, and marries the widow of Hoskuld.

[These dates are reproduced from other editions of this saga, written by Allen French, and by Magnus Magnusson and Hermann Pálsson, to whom all acknowledgements are here made. H.T.]

About
Gunnar of Hlidarend

1. Gunnar the Warrior

In the old days, before the volcanoes turned many fields to stone, there were good crops of grain and hay in Iceland, and grass for all the sheep on the hills. And always in the sea round about there were fish to be got if a man was brisk with the net. Icelanders were hard and busy men, forcing the fields and the hills and the sea to give them food, especially during their short summer before winter's cold and darkness came down on them like a great hand; but they were merry men at feast-times, and loved to make songs and rhymes. There were few rich ones about, in those times, and even the chiefs of the valleys and districts thought it no disgrace to work with their hands in the fields, or sail in the fishing-smacks, or to mend their own weapons. This they often needed to do for they were great fighters when the occasion arose. Wherever there was war, an Icelander would be found, from Trondheim to Miklagard and from Dublin to Spain; these men always gave a good account of themselves and had a name for earning their pay. There was always a master willing to employ them.

One of their greatest fighters was Gunnar of Hlidarend, who first began with the sword but later took to the halberd and made it the most fearful weapon in Iceland. In a land full of brave men, few would dare face Gunnar alone, and those who did seldom spread the tale of the meeting. It had to be told by others. Gunnar was a big handsome man with sharp blue eyes, ruddy cheeks and golden hair, and when he was fighting it seemed that three swords were flailing at once, he was so fast. What is more, if one hand grew tired he used the other, for he was just as able with left as with right. In fact, there was little Gunnar could not do: his arrows never missed their mark; he could jump his own height, wearing his helmet and hauberk; and he could dive and swim like a seal. All told, there were not many in the north as strong, brave and brisk with weapons as Gunnar of Hlidarend, though the island was teeming with fine men.

Gunnar had other qualities comely in a man: he was good-tempered, generous, and always faithful to his friends and family. This was important in Iceland, because when quarrels flared up into feuds friends and families had to keep together or perish.

Now when he was about twenty-five years old and in the fullness of his strength, Gunnar was drawn into such a feud by his kinswoman, Unn.

She was a pretty girl who had married the sea-rover Hrut and had brought with her a dowry of eighty cows; but their marriage did not turn out well. Certainly, Hrut was a real man and a keen warrior; but this was his downfall, for he had fought so well against pirates in Norway that the queen there gave him rich gifts to keep him by her side. And when at last Hrut asked to return to Iceland, this jealous queen laid a spell on him to prevent him from loving any other woman.

For a while after Hrut's ship returned, Unn put up with her husband, whose heart seemed still to be in Norway, but at last she could stand him no longer and went to her father, Mord Fiddle, to complain that Hrut did not love her any longer. Mord Fiddle was furious and demanded his daughter's dowry back again. But he got a cold answer from the sea-rover, Hrut, who told him that he could only have it if he fought for it. Mord was an old man and Hrut was already famous for his sword-play, so there was nothing that could be done at that time. When Mord died, he left everything to his daughter to console her; but Unn, disappointed by her marriage, became a spendthrift and soon ran through her fortune.

And when at last she had nothing left in the world, she went to her kinsman Gunnar and asked him to get her dowry back from Hrut, who now had no right to it, since she was divorced from him according to the common law of the land.

Sitting outside his farmhouse in the sun, Gunnar said, 'I'll give you all the money you need, Unn. But, as you recall, I am a fighting-man, not a lawyer, and I do not know how to sue Hrut for your dowry.'

Unn answered icily, 'I was not thinking of law, but of swords. Hrut thought highly of himself when he challenged my old father to single combat. Now is the time for you to put that cold-hearted braggart in his place.'

Gunnar was not to be caught so easily and shook his head with a quiet smile.

'Very well,' said Unn, 'but I thought I could depend on you. Look, you say you do not know how to bring my case to law; very well, go and see your old friend, Njal of Bergthorsknoll. He is the finest lawyer in Iceland. He will surely tell you what to do.'

After this, it was not long before Gunnar got himself tangled up in the quarrel, which was to bring death to many men before it ended.

Now Njal of Bergthorsknoll was truly the right man to go to, for no one was craftier in legal affairs than he. It was said that any man who followed his advice came out well in lawsuits. He was brave, honest and handsome at this time, about forty years old, and was always busy on his farms, which made him a prosperous chieftain. In manner Njal was always gentle and willing to help his neighbours. Perhaps it was as well that his wife, Bergthora, was a little more harsh-natured for, with six children to rear, more than kindness and legal knowledge are needed. All the same, if Njal had any faults they were these: that at times he could glimpse into the future, and that never in his life had he been able to grow a beard, such as most Icelanders wore on their chin so proudly.

When Gunnar reached the farmstead at Bergthorsknoll Njal welcomed him warmly, for among the Northfolk good friends were always valued and always needed. But Njal's calm face clouded when Gunnar spoke of the dowry-claim.

'This could put your life in danger,' he said at last. 'Yet if you will follow my advice in every detail, things might work out well for Unn. So, pay heed: this is what you must do . . .'

For long, as they sat, Njal's voice sounded on: he told Gunnar to ride towards Hrut's farmstead disguised as Hawker-Hedin the Mighty, a big, surly and quarrelsome fellow, and a wicked breaker of bargains. 'Wear a rough coat over a striped shirt of wool,' said Njal, 'and underneath all that, keep on your good clothes and carry a small axe. Take two trusted men with you, and each of you take two horses—one fat and one lean. On the lean horses, load baskets of rough-made ironware, such rubbish as would cause any customer to quarrel.'

'How will this help Unn?' asked Gunnar, scratching his head.

Njal smiled and said, 'Patience, friend. No man ever caught a fish by rushing into the sea. All along the way to

Hrut's house, keep your hat pulled well down over your face
and behave just as Hedin does: that is, show everyone your
worst articles, all the while praising them highly. And if any
farmer doubts your word, fly into a mock fury, snatch the
spade or bill-hook away and threaten to chop the man down.
If any farmer makes a deal with you, in spite of this, go back
on your bargain and find an excuse to cancel it. In this way,
word will spread before you that Hedin the Hawker is a
dangerous and untrustworthy fellow. Now, don't ride
directly to Hrut's steading: stay the first night at the farm of
his half-brother, Hoskuld, in Laxriverdale. Get up to your
worst tricks there, and before morning Hoskuld will secretly
pass on the word about you to Hrut. Mark my words, it will
not be long before Hrut has you in his house, to see what he
can make of you. He thinks of himself as a great man-tamer,
being a seafarer and pirate.'

'And when I am there,' said Gunnar, 'what then?'

Njal answered, 'Sit on a bench, facing Hrut's chair, and
act like a rough simpleton. Claim to know everything, yet
show that you know nothing. Tell Hrut that there are no
good fighters left in Iceland, and no great lawyers either,
since old Mord Fiddle died. This will interest Hrut, I
promise you. Accuse him of keeping Unn's dowry unfairly,
by challenging her father to fight when he was too old even
to lift a sword. This Hrut is a touchy, proud man, and he will
reply hotly that if Mord was so great a lawyer, he would
have known how to press the claim correctly before the
Althing Court. At this, put on your simplest voice and ask,
"Very well, how should it be done?" And when Hrut tells
you, repeat the words after him, as though summoning him
to court—but see that you keep making small mistakes, in
word or phrase.'

Gunnar sighed noisily. 'Why should I do this?' he asked, confused.

Njal shook his finger and said, 'There is good reason behind it. You see, Hrut will soon begin to think that Hedin the Hawker is an utter fool, and so he will have no suspicions of you. He will teach you the summons, like a man teaching a rhyme to a stupid child. At last, when you have repeated it after him many times, suddenly say it quite correctly, and then ask him if there were any mistakes this time. Hrut will be quite pleased to have knocked something into your thick head, and he will tell you that no flaw could be found in your summons. The moment he says this, you must answer in a low voice, so that only your two companions can hear you, "I make this summons in the law-suit which was put in my charge by Mord's daughter, Unn." '

Gunnar laughed and slapped his thigh. 'I see how this trickery works now,' he said. 'In this way, before witnesses, I shall legally summon Hrut to court!'

Njal nodded. 'Yes,' he said. 'But do not underestimate him: before the night is out, he may see it too. So I advise you to tread warily afterwards. When all are asleep, you and your friends must get up silently, creep out of Hrut's house, and ride away on your better horses. Leave the other ones behind, for they will have served their purpose in carrying your trading-goods on their backs. But one thing more: gallop off beyond the fields and stay up in the hills where Hrut cannot find you. Have no doubt, once he knows you have tricked him, he will come looking for you with his men, and they will bring swords with them.'

Gunnar shrugged his broad shoulders. 'That would not trouble me greatly,' he said.

Njal frowned and said, 'You are not doing this to find a

fight for yourself, my friend, but to get Unn's dowry back. Bear that in mind always, and after you have been three days in the hills and Hrut has grown tired of searching and gone home, you must ride south again to your own farmstead. But don't take the risk of being seen and ambushed. Ride only by night—and if all goes well, when the Althing Court meets this summer, I will be there and will support you in the law-suit. Now let us go in and drink a cup of my wife Bergthora's best ale. It is thirsty work, this talking. Especially to a fellow like you, who needs everything said twice!'

2. Hoskuld's Dream

ALL went as Njal advised and by this trick Gunnar was able
to accuse Hrut in his own house before witnesses, and then
to steal away by night, galloping to the hills on the strong
horses.

But a curious thing happened, just about the time
Gunnar crept away from Hrutstead: Hoskuld, Hrut's half-
brother woke from a troubled sleep and roused his men.
'I have had such a disturbing dream,' he said, 'that I
must tell you of it. In this dream, I thought I saw the
biggest bear in the world leaving this house, with its
two playful cubs, and making its way to my brother's
house at Hrutstead. Tell me, did any of you notice anything strange about the tall surly trader who was here
earlier?'

The sleepy men scratched their heads, trying to remember. Then one of them said, 'Yes, I saw something,
Hoskuld. Under his ragged sleeve, I noticed scarlet cloth
and lace just showing. And once, when he waved his
hands about in anger, I glimpsed a gold bracelet on his
right arm.'

Hoskuld began to buckle on his sword. 'That settles it,' he
said. 'All of you, get ready to ride, for that man was no
common hawker: he could only have been Gunnar of
Hlidarend. And if he is still in my brother's house, we had
best go there also, before it is too late.'

Everyone hurried, carrying swords and axes, and

24

soon they had roused Hrut from his bed and Hoskuld
had told of his dream and suspicions. Suddenly Hrut
gave a miserable sigh. 'If what you say is true, then I have
been outwitted, for I taught that fool of a hawker how to
bring me to law and get Unn's dowry back. Come, let us
look for him.'

But Gunnar was not in the house, nor could they find him
in the hills, although they scoured them for three days.

'It is my belief that Njal is at the bottom of this,' said
Hoskuld. 'No other man would have thought of such a trick.
I'll wager he is well-satisfied with this night's work.'

And truly he was, for Gunnar called in at Bergthorsknoll
and told Njal how all had worked out; and when he heard
the details, a quiet smile passed over his smooth and beardless face.

'All goes well for the moment, my friend,' he said. 'But
the biggest hurdle is still to leap. Now go home and
keep away from Hrut and Hoskuld until the Althing
meets. It would be a shame if you were caught alone on the
hills or in the fields, after all the trouble we have taken
together.'

Gunnar's face flushed. 'I will meet the two of them anywhere,' he said. 'I am afraid of no men in Iceland.'

Njal shook his head. 'That is no news to anyone,' he
answered. 'But we are concerned with law now, not sword-
blows. However brisk you are with the blade, that will not
get Unn's dowry back. Such things must be gone about in
the right way.'

Then Gunnar laughed and clapped Njal on the shoulder.
'You keep me in my place, Njal,' he said, 'and I thank you.
I will do as you say and may our luck hold when we meet at
the court.'

Njal smiled as Gunnar mounted his horse and rode proudly away through the farmyard. 'We shall see,' he said to himself. 'Ah, we shall see. Who can be certain, in this tricky world?'

3. Althing and Longship

THAT summer at the Althing, matters turned out strangely for Gunnar. Hrut protested a little, claiming that though Gunnar had spoken the summons correctly, he had not brought the usual three witnesses to the Law Rock, but only the two fellows who had been with him disguised as pedlars.

Such quibbling angered the big fighter, so now he took the law into his own hands and shouted out, for all the assembled Icelanders to hear, 'Very well, Hrut: if it does not suit you to follow our law obediently, then I will try another way. I call on all present to hear that I give you the same choice that you gave to old Mord Fiddle. I now challenge you to single combat, on the island here in Oxar River, the fight to be fought this very day. If you win, you keep the dowry; but if you lose or refuse to fight then you must restore it to Unn. That is my word.'

Then he turned on his heel and strode back to his booth, while all the Northmen muttered and nodded, staring at Hrut to see how he took this challenge. It was not long before Hrut and Hoskuld turned away, too, and went to their hut. Hrut was furious, and beat his fist against his head. 'I have never refused a challenge in my life,' he said. 'It goes hard with me now to back down.'

Hoskuld put his hand on his brother's shoulder. 'Hrut,' he said, 'if you face Gunnar, you are a dead man. Be advised by me—pay back the dowry.' After a while Hrut nodded grimly and so the two brothers walked to Gunnar's hut and handed over the money. He took it calmly and said, 'This shows my claim was a just one. I hope the money will serve us well.'

Hrut could not contain himself. 'Trouble will be your only reward,' he said, his eyes blazing and his teeth showing.

Gunnar leaned against the lintel, tossing the money-bag in the air and then catching it. 'That is as must be,' he answered, quite unshaken by the threat. 'Have you any more to say?' But Hrut was now speechless.

When they got back to their hut, both brothers were trembling with anger. Hoskuld burst out, 'How can we get revenge on this fellow!' But Hrut, biting his lip, said, 'Perhaps punishment will fall on him from another quarter, brother; and then, who knows, he may even come begging us for help.' They said no more, but waited their time.

And so Gunnar gave back the dowry to his kinswoman, Unn, refusing to accept a penny for his trouble. 'One day,' he said to her, 'I may need your help—and that will be payment enough for me.' Unn smiled and said, 'I will always do what I can, kinsman. I am deeply in your debt.'

All the same, it was not long before Unn married a friendless, bad-tempered man called Valgard the Crafty, without the consent of her kinsfolk. Both Gunnar and Njal were against this wedding and said that no good could come of it. But Unn laughed at their warnings, and in due course she had a son named Mord of Hof. When this boy grew up, he was even more crafty and spiteful than his father, and caused great trouble to his kinsfolk, and especially to Gunnar —without whose kindness he would never have been born. But that is the way of life.

Gunnar's mind was now on other things. A viking ship

from Oslo had landed, and its captain and crew came to stay the winter with Gunnar, for the seas round Iceland were fierce. Over the fire, as storms beat on the shutters, the viking told such tales of his travels round Norway and down into Russia that Gunnar got the itch to sail with him when spring came. So, naturally, he went to Njal and asked if he would look after the farm at Hlidarend while he was away. Njal agreed to this, and so Gunnar and his warrior-brother Kolskegg sailed away with the viking, to see what they could find in the Baltic.

All told, Gunnar was away from Iceland for two years, during which time important things happened, although they did not seem so at the moment.

In Oslo Fjord he borrowed two longships, one forty-oared and the other sixty-oared, sizeable vessels, and with them he roved up and down the waters, fighting other seafarers and gathering great spoil. In these affairs, Gunnar and Kolskegg practised all the old viking war-tricks; such as catching a spear in mid-flight and hurling it back at its owner, or letting the enemy's sword bite into the shield and then snapping it off at the hilt, or jumping on to their opponent's ship and heaving its anchor-stone into the boat-bottom to smash the planks and let the sea come in. Men who met Gunnar face to face never knew how to defend themselves, for his speed was so dazzling that it seemed he had three swords that flamed like the Northern Lights about him. He would often topple his opponent with the leg-blow, after which Kolskegg would come up with a spear and finish the story.

So they roved down to Denmark, then east to Sweden, and at last to the island of Osel which lies off Estonia. It was while Gunnar's ships were anchored there, sheltered by a

headland, that a stranger came scrambling down the rocks
to them and asked to speak to Gunnar. When the two were
together, the man said, 'My name is Tofi, and I have news
for you, shipmaster.'

Gunnar looked at him with searching, narrow eyes and
said, 'I am here; which you can see from my shadow on the
sand.'

Tofi licked his lips and said, 'Aye, it is a long shadow.'

Gunnar frowned and said, 'My sword is nearly as long.'

Tofi spoke fast then and said, 'I am coming to that.
Listen, just over this headland lie two longships dressed for
war, and commanded by two fierce brothers. I doubt if you
have run up against any fighters of their skill before.'

Gunnar smiled and said, 'I have seen a few, here and
there. They have not stayed long to talk with me. Something always took them away.'

Tofi smiled grimly now and said, 'The two I speak of have
always watched the other man go first. One carries a short-
sword that sniffs holes in a man's mail like a stoat after a
rabbit. The other, Hallgrim, swings a halberd which is so
spell-strong that it slashes through any other weapon.
Besides which, it gives off a loud ringing noise when any
man is to be killed by it. I ought to tell you that these
brothers have many more men than you, that they are well
aware of this, and that they mean to sail round the headland
soon and finish you.'

Gunnar nodded and said, 'You interest me. Now, this
halberd, how would you describe it? How long is it, for
instance?'

Tofi wrung his hands and began to glance over his
shoulder. 'I beg you,' he said, 'do not delay. If they catch
you unprepared, as you are, then they will not only kill you,

but you will lose the chance of capturing the great treasure they have hidden ashore here.'

Gunnar walked slowly to the man and clenched a hand on his shoulder. Tofi fell to his knees babbling and said, 'I was going to tell you about it all the time, I swear it.'

Gunnar squeezed a little harder, but not enough to snap a bear's leg, and whispered, 'Of course you were, of course you were. I can read that in your eyes. So, you want me to kill the pirates, and then you will lead me to this treasure, is that it?'

Tofi nodded so hard that the tears splashed on to his knees. 'Yes, master,' he said. 'Of course I did not want it for myself, I am only a poor simple fellow. What would I need with treasure?'

Gunnar lifted him with one hand, absent-mindedly, to his feet and said, 'Aye, what indeed? But I'll play fair with you, you shall be rewarded if what you say is true; and in the meantime, here is a gold ring. If all goes well, it is yours; but if you have tricked me, I shall come back and ask you for it again. It is all right, you will not need it then.'

While Tofi was beating his hands against his head, Gunnar went back aboard his ship and told the men to get ready for a slightly harder fight than usual. They nodded and smiled.

'All's grist that comes to the mill,' said one of them, yawning.

And it was a hard fight. Men fell all over the decks, and the scrubbed white wood soon changed its colour. Gunnar, searching the enemy throng, set eyes on a big man who bore a bright halberd, and made towards him.

'Hey! Are you named Hallgrim?' he shouted, over the battle din.

The viking laughed at Gunnar and called, 'Do you need to ask?'

So Gunnar bared his teeth and pretended to rush forward, holding out his sword. Hallgrim smiled at this and swept out with the long weapon, a blow which would have brought down a charging horse. But Gunnar was not there when it landed. He had jumped back, to let the sharp blade sink itself in the ship's planks. Then, while Hallgrim wrestled to free the bright iron, Gunnar hacked down at his enemy's arm, and though the sword-edge did not bite, the force of the stroke broke the bone, and down clattered the halberd to the deck.

In one breath's space, Gunnar had snatched up the great weapon; in two breaths' space, he had laid Hallgrim stark with its blade.

'Oh,' said Gunnar, casting his sword away, 'you beauty, you! Together we will go through the north and make fame for each other.'

Then he turned, and seeing Kolskegg in trouble with a tall viking, he used the halberd on him from behind, and once more delighted in its balance and sharpness.

After that the battle was soon over, and the men of Gunnar's band gained great prizes—armour and weapons, and even clothing.

Later on, Tofi came to Gunnar and said, 'It was well done. I will lead you to the hidden treasure now.'

Gunnar was fondling his halberd and said, looking up from under his eyelids, 'You need not tremble so, poor simple Tofi; I was not going to ask for the ring back. What I have got here is worth a hundred rings.'

But Tofi led Gunnar to a wood, and there beneath a pile of saplings they found a great hoard of gold, silver, arms and rich clothes. It was far more than Gunnar had expected to find, and he said to Tofi, 'My friend, you have dealt fair with me, so now I will reward you. Tell me what you would like best of all.'

Tofi looked steadily at the big warrior and answered, 'I am a Dane by birth. Vikings captured me and left me on this island. Now, all I beg is to be taken back to my homeland. I do not ask for your gold.'

So Gunnar sailed for Denmark and set Tofi down at Hedeby. That was an easier harbour to get into than out of, for Harald Bluetooth, the King of Denmark, was holding his court there and nothing happened in Hedeby that Bluetooth did not find interesting. And though he was a Christian and had chopped off a hundred heads to prove it, Bluetooth never let his religion stand in the way of a good bargain.

Soon Gunnar found himself sitting beside the Dane-king in the feast-hall, eating and drinking mightily, and leaping down from the dais to wrestle with the Jomsvikings whenever Bluetooth commanded it.

The King watched his champions fall among the rushes, and towards the end of a fortnight of such merriment, he scratched his long red nose and said to Gunnar, 'I could find a place for you among my fighting-men, lad.'

But Gunnar shook his head, smiling so as not to offend Bluetooth, whose rages were well known, especially when his toothache came on, and replied, 'I regret it, my lord, but I have sworn to go back to Iceland to attend to certain business among my kinsmen.'

For a long time, Bluetooth stroked his iron-grey beard. Then he said, 'I have a wife in mind for you, Icelander, and you would do well to let my Bishop marry you to her with-out delay.'

Gunnar wished he had his halberd with him then, but Bluetooth's law was that no edged weapon should be brought to the feast-hall. So in the end, he got away lightly by presenting the Dane with a longship filled with treasure. In return for this, old Bluetooth gave him his own second-best throne-robes, a pair of gloves stitched with gold wire, a headband decorated with gold studs, and a fur cap that had come all the way from Russia.

As Gunnar sailed out of Hedeby the next day, he breathed a sigh of relief and said to Kolskegg, 'Not many flies come so well out of the old spider's web, brother.'

Kolskegg nodded bitterly and answered, 'It has cost us something, but we still have heads on our shoul-ders.'

After that, they sailed north and put in at Trondheim, where Earl Hakon was ruling Norway at that time. At the Yule feasting there, the Earl gave Gunnar a gold bracelet, and was about to offer him the hand of his kinswoman, Bergljot, in marriage, but Gunnar wanted to sail on the spring tide to Iceland.

Earl Hakon took this news better than Bluetooth had done. All the same, he said, 'Last year's harvest was bad in Iceland, they tell me. The trading there will be poor, my boy. Think of that before you go.'

But Gunnar said, 'It is where I belong, my lord, and go I must.'

So Hakon filled Gunnar's ship with flour and sound timber for building with, and sent him aboard with friendly wishes. The Earl was a just man, and set friendship higher than a hard bargain.

Gunnar and Kolskegg thought all the better of him for that, and by good fortune they reached Iceland once more, landing in the estuary near Arnarbaeli in early summer, just before the Althing was due to meet.

4. The Woman in Scarlet

LEAVING the sailors to unload the longship, Gunnar and his brother Kolskegg lost no time in riding over to visit Njal and to tell of their adventures on the sea. Njal listened, smiling, and said, 'Well, now you have proved yourself among men; but do not think that this is the end of it. A hero like you will always find other fighters who will want to test themselves against him, out of envy for his fame.'

But Gunnar laughed and answered, 'I want nothing more than to be friendly with all men, Njal.'

The older man shook his head sadly. 'Perhaps they will not let you,' he said.

So, to change the subject, Gunnar asked Njal if he was going to visit the Althing, but Njal turned his head away and said, 'No, and it would pay you not to go either, my friend.'

This warning fell on empty ears, because Gunnar and Kolskegg had been away so long that they yearned to jostle among the crowds again and to hear all the news of Iceland. So, dressing up in Bluetooth's old throne-robes and wearing the gold bracelet Earl Hakon had given him, Gunnar rode with his brother to the meeting, and was soon the centre of attraction, for all men wanted to hear of his adventures among the vikings.

Later, as the brothers were strolling about for all to get a good look at them, they met a group of young women, the leader of whom took Gunnar's breath away. Her

golden hair hung thickly almost to her waist; her legs
were the longest Gunnar had ever seen; she stood taller
than all her companions, and though there was a haughty
expression on her pale face, she smiled at Gunnar and
called out boldly to him, greeting him and asking how he
had enjoyed his voyage abroad.

This surprised the warrior, because the lovely young
woman was wearing a richly-embroidered red tunic under
a scarlet cloak trimmed with lace, and hardly looked the sort
of person who would start a conversation in public with a
strange man. But Gunnar was never one to miss an opportunity, and so, taking her aside, he told the long story of his
adventures. All the time he was talking, she showed such
interest in him that he felt very encouraged, and said,
'What is your name, lady?'

She looked at him slyly and said, 'I am Hallgerd, daughter
of that Hoskuld in whose house you once stayed when you
were pretending to be Hawker-Hedin.'

Gunnar whistled through his teeth. 'So,' he said, 'the
man I challenged at the Althing, Hrut the Sea-Rover, is
your uncle?'

Hallgerd nodded with a smile and, staring boldly into his
face, said, 'Not all of our family refuse challenges, viking.'

Now Gunnar could not hold back. 'Tell me,' he asked,
'are you married, Hallgerd?'

She paused a little, then said, 'No, I am rather particular
about the men I like.' But she said this with such a smile
that Gunnar took her hand and said, 'Then will you marry
me, Hallgerd?'

She drew her hand away, though not too hurriedly, and
answered, 'If you are serious, then you must ask my father
that question.'

After that, it was not long before Gunnar went to Hoskuld's booth at the Althing, deeply in love with the young woman; and in spite of their old feud, Hoskuld and Hrut received the warrior kindly at their table.

'Look, Gunnar,' said Hoskuld, when they had talked a while, 'my daughter is not the right woman for you. I am bound to tell you this.'

Then Gunnar flared up and said, 'You say that because of our old quarrel. I thought that was all forgotten now.'

But Hoskuld patted his arm and said, 'My friend, what happened years ago has nothing to do with it. Now we all know you to be a brave man and an honourable one—but my daughter Hallgerd is a strange mixture of bad as well as good, and she could bring you unhappiness. I will not deceive you, Hallgerd has already been married twice before, and both times her husbands were killed, merely for correcting her wild ways with a slap on the face, by a blood-thirsty Hebridean called Thjostolf, who doted on her and lived in her house as her foster-father or bodyguard.'

Gunnar said, 'Don't you think I can deal with such a kitchen-ruffian, then?'

Hrut the Rover smiled grimly and said, 'In this, you come too late. I have already put the sword into him myself.'

Gunnar gave a great laugh and cried out, 'Then what are we arguing about? The way is clear for our wedding!'

And though Hoskuld warned him that Hallgerd was wasteful as a housewife, and never forgave anyone who raised a hand against her, the warrior would not listen, and so the betrothal was arranged.

When Gunnar told Njal the news, the wise counsellor shook his head, saying, 'This match will not turn out well,

Gunnar. I foretell that, because of it, much blood will be shed, and even our friendship will be strained.'

But Gunnar still would not listen. 'Never, old comrade,' he said. 'The woman who could part us has yet to be born.'

And so it seemed for a while. After the wedding, to bind their friendship, Gunnar and Njal made it their custom to hold feasts each year, first at one house and then at the other, and these were always merry gatherings because Njal's family were fine people to eat and drink with. His wife, Bergthora, was perhaps a little sharp-tongued at times, but that came of having to rear her three headstrong sons, and usually she was the kindest and merriest of women.

These three sons were the finest brood of hawks to be found in Iceland. Any father in the world would have been proud of them. The eldest, Skarp-Hedin, looked every inch a fighting-man, with his great height, his curly chestnut hair, and his eagle nose. His only fault was his mouth, which made him always seem arrogant because of his large teeth; and certainly he could be very cutting in his speech, if his quick temper was roused. Usually, though, he kept his words under control, and he was popular for miles around because of his skill with weapons, at running and at swimming.

Njal's second son was Grim, and his third Helgi; they were both tall, good-looking youths, with a fine head of dark hair, and great skill in fighting. Since they were all married and living at home, Njal's farm was quite crowded for the feasts.

There was a fourth son, who held the name of Hoskuld, but who belonged to an earlier marriage that Njal had had with a woman called Hrodny. Though this Hoskuld often rode over to Bergthorsknoll to visit his father and his half-brothers, he lived mostly with his mother on a farm at Holt and usually feasted there among his own family. He was a brave man, but was not called on by fate to play a large part in this saga.

Now it happened one year that Helgi and his wife were out visiting when Njal's feast began, so beautiful Hallgerd was given their special place at the table. However, they had scarcely begun to eat when Helgi and his wife came into the hall, at which, Bergthora, being the mistress of the house, asked Hallgerd to move down the board a place and let Helgi's wife have her usual seat on the bench.

For the first time since her wedding, Hallgerd's temper flared like a pine-torch. 'What!' she screamed. 'Do you regard me as an outcast woman? Is this your famous hospitality? Who are you, anyway? Your fingernails are as thick and ridged as a turtle's shell; and, as for your clever husband, he is so small a man that he cannot even grow a beard!'

Bergthora gazed calmly at her guest and said, 'Njal and I find no faults with one another, Hallgerd. As for this matter of beards, your first husband had a well-grown one, but that didn't stop you from having him killed.'

At this, Hallgerd jumped up in fury and shouted at Gunnar, 'Your fame is useless to me if you do not avenge this insult.'

Suddenly Gunnar leaped over the table and stalked towards the door. Turning back he said coldly to his wife, 'I'm for home, and that's where you would be better, Hallgerd. I owe Njal too much to squabble with him because of your childish sneers. Come along, woman. I shall not wait for you.'

Hallgerd followed, with as much dignity as she could find,

but at the door she called over her shoulder, 'We shall meet again, Bergthora.'

Njal's wife glanced up from her platter and said, 'And when we do, it will profit you little.'

In such small ways do great troubles begin. Though Gunnar took his wife home and kept her there the whole of the winter, the seeds of bloodshed had been sown.

5. The Killings

THINGS did not go smoothly after that, for Hallgerd was determined to break her husband's friendship with Njal. Two years running, she sent a housecarle to murder one of Njal's men, as they worked in woods or fields; but each time Bergthora sent a man of her own to get blood-vengeance, with axe or sword. And each time Njal and Gunnar settled the differences between them by paying fines to one another, without putting the case before the Althing, for they were more than ever determined that Hallgerd's spite should not spoil their friendship.

All the same, Bergthora was never content that Gunnar's malicious wife should cause such bloodshed and worry; nor were Njal's three sons—especially Skarp-Hedin, who told his father that such stains could not be wiped out with a fine, however high.

'Our good name is being whittled away like a stick,' he said. 'Two hundred ounces of silver are nothing compared with that.'

But wise Njal held his peace.

Now one day a band of wandering women, great gossips, who walked about Iceland begging or getting work in the hayfields at the right season, called at Njal's farm and then went on to Gunnar's. They were the main spreaders of news in those days, so Hallgerd asked them what Njal was busy at.

The women laughed and said, 'Oh, he's busy sitting still, lady.'

'And what of his sons?' asked Hallgerd curiously.

'Oh, they are burnishing their weapons and dreaming that they are men.'

'Now what are Njal's housecarles doing?'

'One of them is carting manure from the stables.'

At this, Hallgerd gave a shrill laugh and said, 'Good! Njal must put it on his chin, then his beard may grow perhaps!'

There was great laughter in the hall at this, and a loud-mouthed fellow named Sigmund made up a song on the spot, calling Njal 'Old Beardless', and his sons 'Little Dung-Beards'.

Just then, Gunnar strode in furiously, having heard it all, and forbade anyone to repeat the insulting words that had been said under his roof.

But it was too much to expect that this piece of gossip would go unheard; before morning the beggarwomen had slipped out and had told Bergthora, who was as generous with her rewards to them as she was now with her hatred of Hallgerd.

'Well,' she said coldly to her sons, as they lolled round the table, 'what are you going to do about this new insult?'

Skarp-Hedin grinned and said, 'You love flaring up, don't you, Mother! But we are not frantic women, to fly into a rage at everything we hear.'

His mother stood over him and said slowly, 'If you do not avenge this, you will never avenge anything, Little Dung-Beard.' Then she hurried from the room.

Skarp-Hedin smiled again, but this time his brothers

saw that the sweat had burst out on his forehead in beads and that two red spots flamed in his cheeks. All the brothers sat quite still and silent, like images of stone.

That night when Njal was in bed, he heard an axe rattle against the wall-panelling, so he rose silently and looked about the hall. Then he saw that his sons' shields had gone from the wall, so he pulled on his shoes and went outside. The young men were wrapping their cloaks about them and whispering in the darkness.

'Hey,' called Njal, 'and where are you three off to?'

Skarp-Hedin said calmly, 'We just thought we would round up the sheep, Father.'

Njal said, 'And do you need your weapons for that, son?'

Skarp-Hedin shrugged and said, 'Well, you see, if we can't find the sheep, we thought we would do a little salmon-fishing.'

Njal stood and gazed at them firmly for a while, then said slowly, 'If you find a good salmon, see that he does not escape you, Skarp-Hedin.'

When he got back to bed he said to his wife, 'Well, you have started something now.'

Bergthora smiled in the darkness and answered, 'With all my heart, I hope they will bring back news of Sigmund's death because of that poem.'

Then she laughed in the darkness, and even went back to sleep laughing. Njal listened to her half the night, and got to sleep just about dawn-time, at which hour the three brothers reached Gunnar's steading, and rejoiced to see Sigmund come out, wearing his best red clothes, in company with an ill-tempered Swede named Skjold. These two mounted horses and rode to look for a strayed stallion in

45

the hills, so the brothers followed quietly until they dismounted, then ran round them.

Skarp-Hedin gave Sigmund plenty of time to raise his spear and shield, then said, 'If you are not too busy making rhymes, perhaps you would care to defend yourself?'

He let Sigmund have first blow, caught the spear in his shield, then sliced the shaft in two with his sword. With his next stroke, Skarp-Hedin split the man's shield in two, so causing Sigmund to take to the sword. Then, after a little circling, Skarp-Hedin took Sigmund's sword-point into his own shield and with a quick jerk dragged the blade from his hand, so that the man stood unarmed.

While this was going on, the other two brothers put an end to the Swede, Skjold; one sliced off his foot, to bring him down, and the other put the sword in him at exactly the right place.

But Sigmund did not die so quickly. Skarp-Hedin made him wait for three blows; with the first, he got him in the shoulder and jerked him down on to his knees.

'Ah,' he said, smiling, 'I am pleased to see you kneeling before me. In a moment you will be lying flat on your back.'

Sigmund answered, 'That will be my bad luck.'

Skarp-Hedin nodded, then knocked the helmet from his head with the second blow. With the third, he split the head itself, and Sigmund fell flat on his back, clawing the turf with empty hands.

At this moment, one of Hallgerd's shepherds came up and saw this awful happening. Being a simple thrall, he knew better than to interfere when rich warriors were holding a discussion, so he said nothing.

But, seeing him, Skarp-Hedin nodded to him and smiled;

then he swept off Sigmund's head and flung it over to the trembling shepherd.

'Here, my good fellow,' he said, 'take this to your mistress, and ask her if it is the same head that made up the little rhyme that amused her so much.'

As Njal's sons rode back over the hill, the shepherd stood rooted with the dripping head in his hands; and only when the men were out of sight, did he dare throw it away disgustedly, before he ran in terror to tell Hallgerd what had happened.

As for the brothers, they followed the old Icelandic custom, and down beside the Markar River they announced what they had done to the first men they met. This was so that the Althing would know that the killing had been done openly and not, like murder, secretly.

Hallgerd was beside herself with fury; but Gunnar would not be drawn into her schemes, and brought no suit against his old friend.

Once more, he and Njal settled this difference privately, after which Gunnar announced in public that he had no quarrel with Njal's sons, who had been wickedly provoked by Sigmund's rhyme.

'I would have done what they did, wouldn't you?' he said firmly to the villagers. They looked down at the ground, and shuffled their feet, but did not answer.

6. Hallgerd's Theft

ALL the same, things could not go on like this; and there comes a time when every man's luck runs out, like ale from a leaking cask. And this is how Gunnar's luck began to fail.

One winter hay and meat were scarce in Iceland, so Gunnar, who had a good supply, being a thrifty farmer, let all men share his stores until he also ran out. When his barns and larder were empty, he rode to a neighbouring farmer, Otkel, who still had enough and to spare, and offered him a good price for some hay.

Otkel, however, refused to sell, which angered some of Gunnar's followers who suggested that their master should take what he wanted and give the surly farmer the usual market price for it. Gunnar was too big a man for such petty behaviour and waved the suggestion aside. To show how little he cared, he even bought from Otkel an Irish slave named Malcolm, who was in fact a lazy, dangerous and even murderous man, and one whom Otkel had been trying to get rid of for some time.

When Njal got to hear of Gunnar's plight, he willingly sent fifteen horse-loads of hay and five of meat to his old friend's farmstead, and told Gunnar that in future he must never turn to anyone else when he found himself in need.

Now that summer Gunnar fed and entertained a number of Icelanders who were on their way to the Althing-meeting and, what is more, he invited them to call back at his farm on their return journey, to share all he had.

This annoyed Hallgerd, and she lost no time in calling the Irish slave Malcolm before her.

'I know your kind,' she said to him, 'so waste no time arguing with me, man. I want you to go back secretly to your old master's farm, steal all the food you can, especially butter and cheese, and then set fire to the store-room to cover up the theft. Is that clear?'

Malcolm said, 'And what if I don't?' He hated taking orders from a woman.

Hallgerd looked at him through narrowed eyes. 'I shall have you killed,' she said. 'It is as simple as that, fellow.'

Malcolm did as she ordered, and worse. Otkel's faithful dog ran out, knowing Malcolm's scent, and leapt with joy to see him again. The slave dashed out the dog's brains, and then turned for home.

On the way, however, his shoe-string broke and when he repaired it he carelessly left his knife and belt behind, down by the Rang River.

The folk at Otkel's farmstead did not suspect a theft, but put the fire down to the fact that the storehouse was built next to the hot kitchen. Gunnar was not so easily deceived, though; when he saw the feast that his wife laid for the returned guests, he asked her where she had got so much butter and cheese, for he knew how low their stocks had been.

Hallgerd answered with a sly smile, 'I got them from a place which should not trouble you. Besides, my kitchen affairs are no business of yours, however great you are with a weapon in your hand!'

'Why, you thief!' said Gunnar, unable to control himself. As he spoke, he struck Hallgerd hard across the face with his bare hand.

For a while she gazed at him; then, with ice in her voice, she said, 'I shall remember that blow, warrior. In due course it will be repaid, I promise you.'

Indeed, it was the worst blow Gunnar ever struck, and yet it was the lightest.

It was not long before Otkel's men found the knife and belt and knew where to lay the blame for the fire. Gunnar straightway offered to pay twice the cost of the damage, but Otkel refused this and, instead, summoned Gunnar to appear before the Althing like any common criminal.

This was such a blow to his pride that for a while Gunnar almost went out of his mind with fury. In fact, his blood surged so hotly that he called his brother Kolskegg in and all his carles, and said to them, 'This has gone too far. The law-makers, Gizur the White and Geir the Priest, must be on Otkel's side in this. I cannot stand such injustice, my friends, so I shall take the law into my own hands. This must be settled by axe-blows, not words. At the Althing, I will challenge Gizur to combat and you, Kolskegg, will take on Geir. As for the rest of you, you are well able to deal with Otkel and his yelping followers, aren't you?'

The hall rang with their cries for justice, and so the men rode to the Althing with their weapons.

All the same, their anger soon died down when Njal took Gunnar aside and told him to control himself, since all men present knew the truth of the matter and were on his side. Moreover, Gizur and Geir came up to the war-band and swore that they had no part in this affair at all.

'As far as we are concerned, Gunnar,' they said, 'you have acted fairly towards Otkel with your generous offer. We give you leave to judge this case yourself, and to award as much or as little compensation as suits you.'

So, in the hearing of all men, Gunnar awarded Otkel the value of the storehouse and food, but awarded himself exactly the same amount because he had been brought before the court in mockery. Finally, he sent back the slave, Malcolm, saying that such a thieving hound belonged to Otkel and not to himself. There was no house-room for him at Gunnar's steading.

There was great cheering at these words, but the law-givers did their best to calm Gunnar down and to persuade him to shake hands with Otkel after all.

Gunnar answered, 'Never as long as I live. He can find his friends elsewhere. What is more, I advise him to keep out of my way in the future.'

So Gunnar came back from the court with honour; but he was not fated to live in peace for long. That spring, he was out in a cornfield, carrying a seed-basket and sowing his grain. He had laid his short hand-axe and his finely-woven cloak aside, and was bending down to his task without a thought of harm to anyone, when suddenly a horse galloped madly across the field towards him, ridden by a man who was wildly dragging at the reins.

As Gunnar straightened up, he saw that the rider was Otkel, and that the maddened horse was heading directly at him. The next moment, Gunnar was sent spinning backwards, his face slashed open by the rowel of Otkel's spur.

Getting to his feet, he saw that Otkel was followed by a band of seven riders, so, with the blood streaming down his face, he shouted out to them, 'I call you as witnesses. This Otkel not only summoned me to court unjustly, he has now shed my blood without cause, and in my own field, and I without weapons to hand.'

To tell the truth, Otkel's horse had been out of control and he had never meant to ride Gunnar down, but before he could say so, one of his followers, a loud-mouthed braggart called Skamkel, shouted back to Gunnar, 'Aha! But you looked far more fearsome at the Althing, friend Gunnar, when you had that big halberd in your hand!'

Gunnar glared at him through the blood and said, 'You shall see the halberd again, loud-mouth, when we next meet.'

At this, the band spurred off, but not before Gunnar heard Skamkel call out, 'That was a good bit of riding, my friends!' Then they went over the hill laughing loudly, and Gunnar returned to his farmstead, gnawing his lip with fury. As soon as he could, he told his brother Kolskegg what had happened and on Kolskegg's advice they let all the neighbours know, in case a feud flared up now.

As for Otkel and his band, they reached their destination and Skamkel spread it about that Gunnar had wept when the spur cut him. Otkel did not like to hear this lie, but he could not shut Skamkel's mouth and had to abide by what was said. However, he decided that on the return journey he would keep out of Gunnar's way, and would leave his son in the keeping of a friend called Runolf.

Runolf nodded sadly and said, 'That is a wise move. I do not think that you and your son will ever meet again.'

It was not long before Gunnar got to hear from a shepherd about the rumour of his weeping, and when he did his anger bubbled up like broth in an iron pot.

Quietly he buckled on his sword and put on his helmet. Then he saddled his horse and took down his shield from the wall. But as he grasped his great halberd, it sent out a ringing sound and roused Rannveig, his mother. She came from the farmhouse and said, 'Gunnar, my son, I have never seen such anger on your face before.'

He did not answer her, but leaning on the shaft of the halberd, vaulted into the saddle and rode away.

The old woman went back into the hall, where all the farm-folk were talking as they ate and drank. 'Friends,' she said drily, 'the halberd was talking too, when Gunnar rode away.'

Kolskegg jumped from his bench. 'That means something serious,' he said. Then, running to the stable, he saddled his own horse, and snatching up his weapons, took the trail over the hill.

In the hall, Hallgerd clenched her jaw. 'All goes as I thought,' she said. 'Now they will find out if Gunnar is the man to run away weeping when he gets a little scratch.'

All the folk stared at her aghast, for she looked like a white witch as she stood there, her lovely hands on the table, clenched.

7. The Ford at Hof

GUNNAR rode like a madman across Akratongue, on to Geilastofnar, and so over to Rang River and down to the ford at Hof. He knew that all riders must come at last to this ford, for the river was getting to be broad now on its way to the sea.

There were some milking-pens near the ford, and in them women were working. Gunnar slid off his horse and tethered it near these pens, nodding to the women to wish them good day. He had just tied the reins when Otkel's band came thundering down the clay path to the ford. He jumped out from behind the pens, his halberd held forward.

'Hey,' he shouted to the first man, 'here it is! Now see how much you can make me weep!'

It was a blood-spattered battle while it lasted. Gunnar hacked off one man's hand; then he caught Skamkel like a great salmon on the halberd's point, hoisted him in the air, and dashed his brains out on the path. One man flung a spear at him, but Gunnar caught it in flight and hurled it back with such force that it went through that man's shield, his body, and then on to hide its point in the hard ground behind him.

Otkel came at Gunnar, swinging his sword just below the warrior's knee; but his swipe was too slow and Gunnar leapt above the scything blade like a gay dancer, and drove the halberd through the man at the same time.

55

Just then Kolskegg ran up and, roaring with battle-joy, drove in on the swirling onslaught. Together the brothers killed all eight men who had seen Otkel's spur slash open Gunnar's cheek. It was a debt fully paid down by Rang River that day.

A woman milking there gathered up her skirts and ran to the nearest steading, hoping that carles and thralls would come out and put an end to the bloodshed. But no sane man would come forth at her frantic call. This was not a matter for any but blood-bargainers.

All Gunnar said, when he and his brother got home again was, 'Kolskegg, I am getting to be a little worried about my manliness. You know, I don't enjoy killing men the way I used.'

However that might be, when Gunnar went and told his friend Njal of the fight by the ford, the older man said, 'Ah, all folk will praise you for this—but, my dear friend, this is only the start. Now you will have to go on and on, killing all the time. I ask you, what sort of life is that?'

Gunnar fell silent. He knew that it was no sort of life, facing men with swords all his days, leaving them dead behind him, and going on to face still more. In sudden desperation he turned to Njal and said, 'Old friend, tell me what to do. I cannot ask my wife's advice, so I must depend on you. I beg you, help me, Njal.'

Then Njal said gravely, 'Very well, but listen hard. You must never kill more than once in the same family. Nor must you break any settlement which is made on your behalf. If you disobey either of these warnings then, my dear friend, you will not have long to live, I am sorry to say.'

These last words nettled Gunnar, who broke out,

57

'You, who see so much of other men's futures, do you know how you will die yourself?'

Njal nodded gently. 'Yes, Gunnar,' he said. 'I have foreseen it all. And it will be in a manner that no one expects at present.'

Ashamed at his outburst before his old friend, Gunnar rode home then, and waited to be summoned to the Althing Court.

There the verdict was that Otkel's death should be set against Gunnar's deep spur-wound; that no atonement should be paid for such a trouble-maker as Skamkel; but that compensation should be paid for all the other dead men. Luckily, Gunnar's kinsmen contributed enough money to cover this payment immediately; so Gunnar went from that court with credit, and from that time forth decided he would live in peace at home, and would spend his time as a good farmer, tending his fields and his horses and forgetting blood-feuds and weapons.

8. The Horse Fight

Now it happened that Gunnar had a very fine black stallion
which, though young and untried, was busy learning to
fight and looked as though when he was grown he might
be able to take on any horse in Iceland. In the meantime,
Gunnar tended him and trained him, giving to the young
stallion the love that he might have given his wife had she
deserved it.

But so fickle and taunting is life that Gunnar was not
allowed even to enjoy his horse without interference from
others. At this time there was a man named Starkad, who
had three sons and three nephews, all brisk warriors, with
eyes like hawks watching for insults, real or imagined.

This Starkad also had a red stallion, which had a great
name as a fighter and had many times entertained the
rough farmers up and down the land when they gathered
at the fairs.

It was not long before Starkad sent out a challenge to
Gunnar for the two horses to fight. Gunnar protested that
his stallion was too young for combat yet, but said that
he would agree, provided that the fight was not secretly
an excuse for a quarrel between the two families.

Later, he went to Njal and asked him how such a combat would turn out. Njal said slowly, 'You will win it,
but it will be the cause of many deaths.'

Gunnar paced the hall a while, then asked, 'Will it cause
my own death, Njal?'

The wise counsellor looked away and said, 'No, not directly, Gunnar; but it will bring on quarrels in which you will have no choice but to defend yourself.'

When the horse fight took place, Gunnar was there with his brother and with Njal's sons. Skarp-Hedin, as always alert for trouble, said softly to Gunnar, 'I see trouble brewing over on Starkad's side of the fence. Let me handle your stallion, friend, and I will show them that two can play at violence if anything flares up.'

Gunnar patted the fierce young man on the shoulder and answered, 'I am quite capable of showing them that myself, firebrand; but I do not wish for a quarrel if it can be avoided.'

Gunnar was dressed in his best red tunic and a broad silver belt. He held a goad in his hand, and looked every inch a rich farmer-lord. As for the goad, he did not need to use it, because as soon as the stallions scented each other they ran forward and began to bite and kick, providing the crowd with exciting sport.

But there was one of Starkad's sons and one of his nephews longed to tumble Gunnar into the mud in his best clothes, and when their stallion made the next rush, they added their weight to his rump, hoping to have the famous warrior down before the shouting people. Gunnar was too old a bird to be caught that way, however, and adding his own great strength to that of his horse, he had the others down instead, and, what is more, their horse on top of them, all rolling in the mire.

The young men, hearing the farmers laughing at them, were beside themselves with fury. Leaping up, they rushed at Gunnar, but he sidestepped them easily and flung Kol, Starkad's nephew, to the ground so hard that he fell senseless. Starkad's son, Thorgeir, now vented his anger on Gunnar's stallion, striking out and blinding him with a goad. So it was Gunnar's turn to fly into a fury, and with a blow of his own goad he laid Thorgeir flat on his back.

Kolskegg, Gunnar's brother, took pity on the wounded horse and swiftly put him out of his misery.

But all was in an uproar, for the assembled farmers had not thought to see such a fierce scuffle that day. Thorgeir, rising to his feet, seized his weapons and made for Gunnar, but several bystanders held him by the arms.

Then Skarp-Hedin moved through the crowd, his big teeth showing through his drawn-back lips, until he stood alongside his friend Gunnar. Looking over everyone's head, he said airily, 'This scuffling wearies me. In my opinion, men should use proper weapons, not horse-goads.' As he spoke, his right hand edged towards his sword.

But Gunnar stood still and did not give the signal, while Njal did his best to calm Starkad's family down. No more blows were struck, but it was clear to all that this was but the start of the affair.

Months later, Gunnar met his brother-in-law, Olaf the Peacock, and they ate and drank together; but before they parted, Olaf said quietly, 'If I were you, Gunnar, I should never travel without company from now on. There are those who are waiting to do you harm. I will say no more.' Njal gave him the same warning, and offered always to let his sons ride with Gunnar whenever he left his farmstead.

All the same, Gunnar was not the man to get other folk involved in his quarrels if he could help it; so the upshot was that when he next wished to go on a journey, he took only his brothers, Kolskegg and Hjort, with him, and did not call out Skarp-Hedin as he really should have done. This was a bitter mistake as it turned out.

At Knafahills, with thirty men, Starkad lay in wait, knowing that in such wild country his band would be on Gunnar before he could prepare to meet them.

Now as Gunnar and his brothers got closer, a great tiredness came over the warrior and when they paused for a while near Thjors River, he fell fast asleep. His brothers watched over him, saw that he was tossing and restless, and nodded to one another. When he woke, Kolskegg asked, 'What have you been dreaming, brother? We saw that something troubled you.'

Gunnar looked at him with strange wild eyes and answered, 'Such a dream that, if I had had it before setting out, I should have brought many men with me on this journey.'

When they pressed him for an answer, he went on, 'I dreamed I was riding past Knafahills when a pack of wolves came out at me from all sides. We fought them off, but they were so many, and clustered so close, that I could not get my bow up to skewer them. You and I fought side by side, Kolskegg, but they dragged Hjort away from us and ripped his chest open. Then, in my dream, rage so overcame me that I ran at the wolf who held Hjort's heart in his jaws and, with one blow of my halberd, I sliced him in two, just behind the shoulders. After that, the others ran away.'

When he had finished he turned to Hjort and said, 'I should feel happier if you rode back home immediately, brother.'

But Hjort grinned and said, 'You cannot be rid of me that way, Gunnar. Where you are, I shall be. We set out together, and together we shall stay.'

There was no more to be said; so they rode on.

They had not gone far when needle-eyed Kolskegg said suddenly, 'Look, do you see the light glittering on something, behind those hillocks? They can only be spear-points, brother.'

Gunnar nodded. 'I have seen them,' he answered like a man asleep. 'My dream is coming true.'

Kolskegg said, 'They are a great number, well over twenty, I would say. Do you mean to turn back?'

Gunnar said, 'No man shall ever say I turned back from anything. Let us ride down to Rang River and take our place on the tongue of land that juts into the water. That will make them attack where we want them, not where they want.'

As the three brothers rode down, Kol, Starkad's nephew, stood up from behind his cover and yelled, 'What, are you running away, Gunnar?'

Kolskegg shouted back over his shoulder, 'You can ask that again at the end of the day, loud-mouth!'

No sooner had the brothers got into position on the headland, than Starkad's men rushed down the hill at them. Gunnar, who was no mean hand with the bow, sighted one of the enemy and let fly an arrow at him. It was a good shot, with a high curve to it, but true. The shaft pierced that man's small round shield, went through his eye, and came out at the nape of his neck.

Gunnar's second arrow was even more effective; it went through a man's stomach, and when he fell another tripped over him, at which Kolskegg threw a heavy stone which brained the over-balanced man.

These three hits upset Starkad, as well they might. He said, 'Gunnar is a bit too handy with that bow. Get up close to him so that he can't use it.' Then the rush began again.

Gunnar fought differently now, with the halberd in one hand and his sword in the other. Thorgeir, Starkad's son, called out from the throng, 'Hey, Gunnar, I promised my sister I would bring her your head back.'

It was meant to be a joke. Gunnar answered, 'Good! Come a bit closer, you can't reach it from that distance!'

Thorgeir said to his brothers and cousins, 'Right, let us get round him and crowd him.' So they came on, and the sword in Gunnar's hand did good work. A head flew off even at its first sweep.

Kol, Starkad's nephew, roared out that he wanted to try a blow or two with Kolskegg, and indeed was lucky enough to push his spear through Kolskegg's thigh; but the wounded warrior swung round and took off Kol's leg at a blow.

'Did that land or not?' asked Kolskegg sweetly. 'I didn't really notice.'

Kol, amazed, balanced for a moment on one leg, staring down at his stump on the ground.

'You don't need to stare so,' laughed Kolskegg, 'your leg is really off, I assure you!'

Kol did not answer this, but fell dead to the turf.

And Gunnar was busy all the time. He hoisted Kol's vengeful father on the halberd like a big fish, and hurled him into Rang River, with a hole in his stomach that spoiled his appetite for ever.

Hjort did brisk work, also; but after he had quietened two of the foe, a third came up like the wolf in the dream, and slashing his chest open, killed him instantly.

This was too much for Gunnar to bear; in screaming fury, he swept out the halberd and sliced that man in half; then he flung his weapon from him like a spear and pinned yet another enemy to the ground.

And so it went on, until Starkad shrank back in amazement. 'Back, back, fellows,' he shouted to those who were still standing. 'These are not men we are fighting.'

Gunnar laughed high in his throat and said evenly to Starkad, 'Don't go so soon. You will feel ashamed to say you were in a fight if you have nothing to show for it. Ah, I see you are determined. Very well, I will give you something to take home as proof that you met me.'

So, leaping forward, he slashed both Starkad and Thorgeir with the halberd. They did not wait to take another gift with them.

In all, that day Gunnar and his brothers killed fourteen of their ambushers, and wounded most of those who got away from Rang River.

And when all was quiet again, Gunnar and Kolskegg hoisted dead Hjort on to his shield and rode home, where they buried him under a cairn of stones, and all men mourned this handsome, pleasant youth, who had had little time to enjoy his manhood before the sword took him.

But this wasn't the end of the feud started at the horsefight; there was yet more to come.

At the Althing, Gunnar paid all his blood-fines on the spot, on Njal's advice; but his anger still stayed with him because of Hjort's death, and a few days later he went with Skarp-Hedin and dug up all the bodies of the ambushers and tumbled them about the turf like carrion, for in his opinion they had put themselves outside all law by their cowardly attack.

This action offended Thorgeir, Starkad's son, as much as the wound he still carried from the halberd, and he thought long into the night about how he could bring down Gunnar. Now envy ate his heart and one or the other of them must soon be dead if Thorgeir was to get any sleep again.

9. The Vengeance of Thorgeir

It is fortunate that no man knows what the future holds for him. If Gunnar had known, he would never have fallen in love with Hallgerd's beautiful face at the Althing; nor would he have gone to the horse-fight.

Thorgeir, gnawing his knuckles raw for vengeance, at last got to hear that Njal had foretold Gunnar's death if he killed twice in one family and then broke the settlement imposed on him by the court. So it was not long before Thorgeir, son of Starkad, made friends with his namesake, Thorgeir son of Otkel, a simple, honest and good-hearted fellow. Thorgeir Starkad's son put Thorgeir Otkel's son under an obligation to him by giving him a valuable gold-inlaid spear. Such a weapon-friendship could not be broken lightly in the north in those days, as the crafty giver knew.

Gunnar's brother-in-law, Olaf the Peacock, got wind of this new friendship and soon warned Gunnar of it. 'Look,' he said to Gunnar one day, 'I know you wouldn't hear of another man coming to your aid, but I am going to give you a great hound to guard you. His name is Sam, and once he has taken to you, he will let no one come near you while he has a fang in his head.'

Gunnar smiled and agreed. To tell the truth, Gunnar was the sort of man that animals liked on sight, and it was not long before Sam adored him and followed him everywhere. In fact, the men of Iceland soon began to talk of this great love of the warrior and his hound and, when the story reached Thorgeir's ears, he knew that he would never get his revenge on Gunnar while Sam remained alive.

As the autumn haymaking time came near, Thorgeir son of Starkad gathered twenty-five hard fighters about him and laid bare his plan—that they would attack Gunnar as he sat at home alone, all his workers and carles being down at the river-isles turning the hay. Luckily, Njal got to hear of this and warned Gunnar; but fate does not let go so easily. Some time later, Gunnar and Kolskegg were riding back from the isles after haymaking when, beside Rang River, Gunnar suddenly said, 'Look at my halberd, brother! It is streaming with blood. This foretells a great fight, according to the old legend about this weapon.'

He had scarcely finished speaking, when Kolskegg shouted out, 'Take care, brother, I see men hiding by the riverside.'

'Quick,' answered Gunnar, 'if we gallop, we can perhaps reach the ford and there we stand a better chance of holding them off.'

Setting spurs to their horses' sides, they rode hard, and outstripped the ambushers; then, back to back, the brothers swapped blows with all who came against them, causing so much death among the enemy that at last Thorgeir, Starkad's son, decided to put his plot into action. Going up to Thorgeir, Otkel's son, he bellowed in the youth's ear, 'What, you coward! This Gunnar killed your father, and yet you still let him live. I would be ashamed of myself, if I stood in your shoes.'

The youth, who had fought bravely in the press, flung

back his hair and answered, 'Just watch what I shall do, and then taunt me if you like.'

Jumping in, the youth drove his spear through Gunnar's arm. Gunnar felt the pain right enough, but at that time he was dealing with another man who was as troublesome as a gnat in summer. When he had crushed this gnat, he gave his attention to the youth, who was coming on yet again. The halberd went in like a fish-spear, and soon the youth's limp body floated down the lazy river, until it caught on a boulder and stayed for all to see that life had left it.

Thorgeir, Starkad's son, laughed to himself in the thick of battle, for now he had caused Gunnar to kill twice in the same family. Putting on a grave face, though, he shouted out to his men, 'Come away, fellows. It is not our good day, it seems. Let us see what is for dinner.'

As they retreated, Kolskegg suggested that Gunnar should pick Thorgeir off with a well-aimed arrow; but Gunnar shook his head.

'Brother,' he said smiling, 'you must be out of your mind! We shall have no money left by the time we have paid compensation for those we have killed already! Why, they lie as thick on the ground as my autumn hay.'

Kolskegg answered gravely, 'You have money enough, brother. And I warn you, this Thorgeir will never give up until he sees you dead, if you do not finish him now.'

Gunnar wiped the blade of his halberd. 'Oh, be quiet, you raven,' he said smiling. 'There would need to be several of his sort in my path before I began to tremble.'

When they got back to the steading, Hallgerd was full of joy about the battle; but Rannveig, Gunnar's mother, shook her grey head and said, 'You fought well, my sons; but no good will come of your victory.'

As it turned out, Rannveig was right. At the Althing, the court was most severe against Gunnar, who by this time had got the reputation of killing rather too many men too often. At first, the court considered outlawing him and confiscating all his goods and property; but Njal spoke up cleverly for the warrior and persuaded the jurymen to be a little more lenient. The upshot was that they brought in this verdict: that Gunnar and Kolskegg should leave Iceland for three full years, and that they should also pay blood-fines for the men they had killed.

Gunnar was upset at this sentence, but Njal shook him and spoke to him as though he was a stupid lad.

'Don't be a fool, Gunnar,' said the old counsellor. 'You have killed twice in the same family, which I have often warned you against. Now you still have a chance to come out of this alive, so take it. Pay the fines, and go away for three years. I will look after all your farm-stock until you return, but go. If you break this settlement, nothing can save you.'

Gunnar nodded at last, then smiled and said, 'You are the best friend a man ever had, Njal. You are the one to bring me to my senses, addled as they are! I will obey the judges and will sail abroad for three years, as you say. Come, let us go back to the court and pay up.'

Njal was overjoyed at the way Gunnar took it all and slapped him on the back, greatly relieved. 'I can see that you will yet gain great glory and live to be an old man,' he said.

Perhaps Njal should not have spoken so, for there are always evil spirits listening at such times, only too anxious to make men break their word and fall discredited to the dust.

Whatever the case, that summer Gunnar, Kolskegg, and Gunnar's kinsman, Thrain Sigfusson, got ready to leave on an Oslo-bound longship. Njal's sons, Grim and Helgi, also got ready, being anxious to forage abroad and see what the world was like outside Iceland, which, to tell the truth, was a land that could grow tedious to a brisk young fellow who longed for real adventure.

Outside his crowded farmyard, Gunnar embraced everyone, thanked his men for all their good work, and then revealed with a sad expression that he had made up his mind never to return to Iceland.

The folk cried out at the shock of this unexpected fare-well, and begged Gunnar not to take his banishment so hard. After all, they said, most men of any note in Iceland had been banished at one time or another. It was almost a sign of manhood, they argued; just something that happened, like a bad harvest.

'That is as may be,' said Gunnar, gazing down at the saddle. 'But as for me, I have seen enough of the place. There is a moment when every man comes to the end of his tether—and I have come to mine. Good-bye.' He spoke as though some other put the words into his mouth.

Now a strange thing happened; as the band of riders made their way down towards the Markar River, silent because of Gunnar's black mood, his horse suddenly stumbled, causing him to fall from the saddle and to roll on the ground.

Everyone waited for him to mount again, but instead he still lay there, gazing back up the hill towards his farmstead.

'Are you all right, brother?' asked Kolskegg, spurring back towards him.

Gunnar did not look at him, but almost under his breath, he said, 'Oh, my hillside fields, how lovely they are! How rich and well-kept! Look at that corn, golden and heavy in the ear; and smell that new-mown hay! It has never seemed so sweet before. Why have I been so blind to its beauty? Why did I set such store by the halberd when there was such a farmstead to rejoice in?'

Kolskegg leaned down from the saddle and held out his hand. 'Come on, brother,' he said sternly, 'now is no time for day-dreaming. The ship tugs at the anchor-stone, and we must catch this tide.'

But Gunnar only said, 'Oh, you precious, precious wheat! Oh, you scented hay fields! No, if the fiend had me, I could not leave you.'

Now Kolskegg was angry. 'Stop playing the fool, brother,' he barked. 'I know you don't mean it, but if you did break the court's verdict, it would mean your death, as Njal has foretold. So get up and let's be off.'

Then Gunnar looked at his brother with such strange eyes that even brave Kolskegg shrank back, aghast. 'Why,' Kolskegg whispered, 'you can't mean it! You can't break your oath in this way. Look, you swore to leave Iceland; if you break that pledge, wherever I may be, I shall expect every day to hear of your death. I beg you, brother, get up and ride.'

Now Gunnar rose lazily, a smile on his big rough features. He plucked a grass stalk and put it between his teeth and chewed on it. 'Oh, Kolskegg,' he said, 'this was meant to happen. For the first time in my life I am being shown the beauties of the ordinary world about me.

You and I have spent too long in feuds and bloodshed. We have blinded ourselves to all but swords and spears and halberds. We have spilled other men's blood when we should have been spilling our own tears at the beauties of nature. Come down off your horse and let us learn to live again, forgetting feuds and war-play. Let us be poets, let us live like human creatures and not wild ravening beasts.'

But Kolskegg drew away, putting spur to his horse's flank. Over his shoulder he called back in horror, 'I shall never come back to Iceland. You will soon be dead, and so there will be nothing for me here. Good-bye.'

He galloped off then, to catch up with the other voyagers. When they were out of sight, Gunnar sighed and strolled slowly back to his steading.

Hallgerd ran to meet him, her arms outstretched. 'How glad I am that you have thought better of that foolish trip,' she said. 'Oh, now I have a man to be proud of. How sweet our life will be together, Gunnar.'

Gunnar's mother came out of the farmstead next. When she saw her son, she started as though a bodkin had been thrust into her heart. Then, turning away, she flung her black shawl over her head, as though she did not wish to see him ever again, almost as though he was already a ghost and she was at his mourning.

And she was not the only one to feel this way. As winter came on, the carles and farm-workers silently left the steading, until at last Gunnar was alone, sitting by the dying fire, lost in his dream. That winter, he was the loneliest man in Iceland; perhaps the loneliest man in all the world.

This much is to be said for Iceland law, that harsh it

may be, but it is reasonable; and no man, having sworn to hold to it, can break it and still be reckoned worth a candle. To break that law is to be held of no value, to be outside all consideration, to be *nithing*. And whoso is declared *nithing* had best tie a stone to his legs and leap into Rang River at the full flood, for he will be happier so than as a ghost among reasonable men.

So it was with Gunnar. Hallgerd's sweet words were empty to him now, and her love weighed no heavier than a feast-day ribbon. Rannveig never spoke to him, but flitted from dairy to kitchen like a shadow, as though he had already gone from her life.

Olaf the Peacock, alone of men, saw how it was, and sent messages that he would like Gunnar and Hallgerd to leave their steading and live with him, where they might be safe. At first, Gunnar laughed and said they would go; but then his heart grew heavy again and he forgot about Olaf's offer and went once more to sit by the white ashes and to dream of the past.

Not even the sight of his young son, Hogni, could draw him out of this blind black mood; so at last all folk left him alone, as a bullock is left alone before the butcher comes for him with the pole-axe.

Only the law still remembered him. At the summer Althing, the great law-givers, chiefs and priests, gathered together, every man of note in the whole land, and they agreed that Gunnar was now beyond human aid; that he was an outlaw, a wolf's head, and must be destroyed as a wolf must be, for the good of the community. A band of forty men, some of them old enemies, shook hands and pledged themselves to uphold the law by putting an end to him. Among them was Mord of Hof, son of Unn whose dowry Gunnar had won back many years before, and who, but for Gunnar, would never have been born.

Only Njal still stood by Gunnar, and rode secretly to the steading to warn his friend of what had been decided at the court.

'I beg you,' said Njal, the tears in his eyes, 'let my sons, Skarp-Hedin and Hoskuld, come and stay with you. They will defend you to the death. It is a pity that Helgi and Grim have sailed away.'

Gunnar smiled and shook his head. 'I want none of your good sons to die on my behalf, old friend,' he said.

Njal thumped one hand into another to stress his words. 'But I tell you,' he went on, 'if you are killed, my sons will try to avenge you anyway. They are so devoted to you, they think you are the greatest hero Iceland has ever had. Let them come and keep watch for you, Gunnar, at least.'

But Gunnar only smiled as he took the old man's dry hand and held it a while, to show the love he bore for him. At last, in the dim room, he said, 'In my lifetime, old Njal, many men have died because of me. I want no more of that. But what I would ask you is this—will you look after my son, Hogni, if by any chance anything should happen to me?'

Njal promised this, then, too sad for further words, rode out of the steading and so home to Bergthorsknoll.

After that, Gunnar smiled grimly, as though a god had entered into him, to make him different from all other men. And through that summer and into the autumn, he put on his best clothes, and rode his horse to all gatherings and assemblies, as though tempting men to kill him. But no one raised a finger towards him. One would have thought he was forgiven, but that would not have been

THE VENGEANCE OF THORGEIR

true. They were all waiting, waiting until the time they had decreed, to put an end to him.

This time was haymaking time. For Gunnar the hay-making had always been a crucial time, but never more so than now.

The law avengers, led by Gizur the White and Geir the Priest, rode towards Gunnar's steading, and first they enticed Sam the hound into a sunken lane before the farm, and there they drove an axe into the dog's head, so that he fell dead with a mournful howl.

Inside the house, Gunnar heard this death-cry and said, 'Alas, Sam, my beloved, they have treated you harshly for my sake. I think that my turn will come next.'

Gunnar's farmhouse was built of wood, with windows near the roof-beams, and heavy shutters to cover them. Gunnar was in the loft above the hall when the avengers came.

At first they did not know where he was, so a man climbed up the roof to look in at one of the windows. Gunnar, waiting silently, let this man get half-way through the window before poking the halberd-point into his stomach. The man toppled to the ground, but, amazingly, got up and walked steadily towards Gizur and the other chiefs.

'Is Gunnar at home, then?' asked Gizur.

The man gazed at him quietly, a smile on his white lips. 'That is for you to find out,' he said. 'But I certainly know where his halberd-point has been.' Then he fell flat on his face, stone dead.

Now the hunt was on. Men ran everywhere, howling like hounds for the outlawed wolf. Gunnar got his bow and sheaf of arrows and picked them off the roof when he could sight them. At first he was lucky, and drove them back; but they came again and again, three times.

Now Gunnar had a strange whim. He saw one of his enemies' arrows lodged in a roof timber, and thought idly that it would be a good idea to shoot it back at them, and so wound one of them with his own weapon.

His mother, Rannveig, came into the loft just then and said, 'Don't be a fool, son. They are like hornets, quiet until you stir up their nest. Do not stir them up, I beg you.'

But Gunnar waved her aside and reached out for the arrow, which he let fly and which by chance struck down a man. Yet he had the worst of the bargain, for sharp-eyed Gizur said, 'There he is, in the loft, men. I saw his arm, wearing his gold bracelet, come out to up pick that arrow. Now we shall get him.'

At this, Mord of Hof suggested first that they should burn the house down, with Gunnar in it. Then, when Gizur forbade such wicked action, Mord suggested that they should drag the roof off, to which all agreed.

So they fetched ropes and, slinging them over the outside roof-beams, dragged the whole roof off, leaving Gunnar uncovered for everyone to see.

Still he fought on, and at last some of the avengers began to think of burning him out as one does a wasp's nest, though Gizur the leader was angry at this suggestion, for it was held to be a cowardly way of settling a fight, since fire is the common enemy of all men and of all creatures.

So, for a while, they tried other ways. Men clambered up on to the house wall and slashed at Gunnar. One of them had the good luck to cut his bowstring, so causing him to go back to the halberd.

With his famous weapon he did great damage and, all told, wounded eight men and killed two outright.

Then, in a lull when the enemy were getting back their breath, Gunnar turned inside the house to Hallgerd, his beautiful, wicked wife.

'Woman,' he said, 'I stand a chance of coming through this unscathed, if only I can string this bow again, since it is a better weapon for fighting on house-tops than my halberd is. Let me have two locks of your long hair, and help my mother to plait them into a bow-string for me. It is an old trick which has often worked. I do not see why it shouldn't work today. Odin knows, I need all the luck I can get at this moment!'

Hallgerd was standing across the beams away from him, where he could not reach her. She smiled and said, 'Tell me, husband, does anything special depend on whether or not I cut off my pretty golden hair for you?'

Gunnar laughed and said, 'Special! I would think so. Indeed, my whole life depends on it, and I would call that special just now.'

Hallgerd sheltered behind a beam and said softly, 'In that case, let me remind you of the blow you once gave me in the face, before a crowded hall. No, I shall keep my hair, whether you live or die, dear husband.'

Gunnar turned away and said grimly, 'To each his way of earning fame. I do not ask twice.'

Rannveig, who was in earshot, said, 'I shall not forget your shame, you evil witch. I shall remember your words, make no mistake.'

While they were talking, men swarmed silently up to the top wall, and now they clustered about Gunnar like hounds about a winded stag. He slashed eight of them so deeply that afterwards they hardly breathed, but others came, and then others, until even Gunnar stopped roaring like a lion, and staggered against the rafters, fighting for breath and hardly able to hold up the long halberd.

So, as he lurched back and forward, the avengers struck blows at him from a safe distance, opening his body up in many places and causing his blood to rain down into the house. He snarled like an old lion at each blow, but never asked for mercy, nor even spoke words of any sort that men could understand.

Once they had him down, but when they stood back to examine his body, he struggled up again and went on swinging his halberd, though now so feebly that a playful child might have snatched it from his strange white hands.

And in the end they got round him and killed him, up there on the stark roof, and straightway there were many present who wept to think what they had just been forced to do by the law of Iceland.

Even Gizur said, 'It was not easy to put an end to such a great one. His last stand will be remembered as long as this island still rides above the northern waters.'

Then the chief went over to Rannveig and asked gently, 'May we bury our dead on your land, lady?'

The old woman gazed at him coldly and answered, 'I would be happy if you might all be buried here.'

So Gizur bowed his head and called on his men to withdraw and to do no more damage at Gunnar's steading, for enough harm had been done already.

Indeed, now that he was dead, Gunnar was mourned by all Iceland, as is the way when a hard-faced hero has gone under the ground. Those who envied him when alive, weep bitter tears at the emptiness that comes across the land when he is dead.

Gunnar lived hard and died hard. He never asked for mercy, though he sometimes gave it when it was least expected. Though he put an end to his enemies without looking again at their stark bodies, he came close to weeping when his young stallion was maimed by Thorgeir's spiteful goad. What is more, his hound, Sam, took to him straightway and died for him in the sunken lane with only one howl, and that the brutish axe would have drawn from any creature, were he as brave as a mountain. What is best, this Gunnar paid all his debts, and never had to be asked twice by friend or foe. He might not have died when he did, if it had not been for the horse fight. He certainly would not have died when he did if it had not been for his beautiful wife, Hallgerd. In such matters, even the strongest, the bravest, the most resolute of men are as nothing against the gentle treachery of womankind.

But this be always remembered, Gunnar was a real man, and there have been few such in the world since God first made it; and those few lived mainly in the north, where they can grow, by some accident, as solid through as an oak-tree.

Njal of Bergthorsknoll

10. Ill-met by Moonlight

GUNNAR was dead; but the world does not stop turning because one man has gone, however great he was in life. Those who are left behind must carry on, and, when their grief is over, get about their work again.

All the same, it was long before the memory of this stark warrior faded in Iceland, where all men mourned him deeply, and even his killers started if a footstep sounded behind them, or fell silent in the hall at night if an owl hooted outside in the darkness.

Rannveig, his mother, had a burial mound raised for her dead one, and inside this howe his friends sat the slain warrior upright, to be ready one day if Odin called him out again. But Rannveig would not let his halberd be buried with him in the old manner. She said that it still had work to do and would not even allow anyone to touch it.

'No man,' she said sternly, 'except he who is strong enough to avenge my dead darling, shall ever lay a finger on its shaft.'

It was clear to all men then that the old mother nourished thoughts of vengeance in her stony heart.

Hallgerd the Beautiful learned this earlier than most, for Rannveig, who was a powerful creature, a viking's mother, treated her so harshly, striking at her whenever they met, that soon the woman ran away, glad to have escaped with her life.

'Good riddance to bad rubbish!' screamed Rannveig after her, from the steading door. 'You caused my son's death, and you shall suffer for it, one of these days.'

Hallgerd did not stop to answer the sharp-tongued old woman.

As for Njal, he too was deeply wounded by the death, but there was nothing he could do, since Gunnar had been an outlaw when he was killed, and an outlaw was no more than a rat, and not as much as a cat, in the eyes of the Althing.

As for Gunnar's brother, Kolskegg, who was still away voyaging when he heard of Gunnar's death, he gave up heart and decided never again to return to the cold Northland. Instead, he took the route southwards to Miklagard, along the great rivers and over the weirs, to offer his sword to the Emperor there, and to fight for the Christian God.

Gunnar's son, Hogni, stayed on at Njal's steading and was always going about with fierce Skarp-Hedin, mulling over the past, talking about his father's greatness and death. When the two young men were together, roaming the hills and whispering, fingering their swords and spears, it seemed that Gunnar was still alive in their hearts, as though his spirit had passed into them.

One night a strange thing happened. The two friends were standing near Gunnar's burial-mound in the bright moonlight, when suddenly the top of the howe seemed to rise like a door, and the ghost of Gunnar stood up facing the moon. He was bathed in light, and his grim face was even smiling. Hogni and Skarp-Hedin stood rooted, to see their hero rise from the earth again, and hardly a breath passed their lips as Gunnar's voice began to chant:

86

No man could ever say that I was ungenerous, Hogni.
No, son, I handed out wounds as some lords do rings
And never counted my gifts! Tall as an oak in my helm,
I asked no mercy, son. No, rather death than that!

When the ghost had finished, it sank down and the mound closed in the bright, silver light. Skarp-Hedin turned to his friend and said, 'This is past believing! Dead Gunnar was trying to send us a message. He wants us to know that the fight is still to go on, as far as he is concerned.'

Hogni nodded, hard-faced like his father, and said, 'Yes, still to go on; but I shall need a little help, brother.'

Skarp-Hedin took his hand in the moonlight and said low, 'You never need to ask me, brother. I am two steps ahead of you.'

That night they got ready to go. As Hogni took down the halberd from its iron hooks in the wall, it gave out a ringing sound, and old Rannveig jumped from her bed in a fury.

'What are you doing with that, Grandson?' she demanded. 'I forbade any man to touch it.'

Hogni grinned and said, 'I thought of taking it to my father. He may need it, where he is going, in Valhalla. There is always a certain amount of activity up there, you know, Grandmother.'

The old woman clutched his arm and said fiercely, 'Carry it, my love, and see that it takes good news to your father when you put it into his hands at last.'

As Hogni and Skarp-Hedin went through the darkness, two ravens flew low, just over their heads, all the way. It was as though they knew.

The first farm they came to belonged to two men who had helped kill Gunnar, so the friends decided they would

make a game of what they had to do, and drove all the sheep from the surrounding fields in a great flock right up to the steading walls. There was such a shouting and a baa-ing that night!

Then out came the two farmers, calling, 'What's going on? Why are the sheep up here when they should be down on the pasture?'

Busily they began to beat at the confused animals, turning them, trying to shepherd them back where they had come from.

Then up stood Hogni and Skarp-Hedin. 'Oho!' they called out in the dark, 'and where are you two going, dear friends?'

The startled farmers stopped in their tracks and felt for their swords.

Skarp-Hedin pushed his way through the frightened flock and said, 'Yes, yes, you guessed right! It is just as you thought!'

Then he cut one man down, while Hogni used the halberd on the other. It was quickly done; far quicker than baking a loaf, though not so clean.

They slapped each other on the shoulders in joy and sent the poor sheep scattering, then they went up the hillside road to their next call.

Now for Starkad and his son, Thorgeir.

First, Skarp-Hedin got on to the steading roof and began to tear the thatch off, like a beast munching at it, like one of those trolls of Norway who noisily gobble up the thatch, not eating it politely with a closed mouth.

Everybody inside was soon awake! Everybody was accusing everybody else of letting the sheep stray over the brow of the hill on to the roof. And everybody was saying,

'No, certainly not! I put the latch on the gate when I came to bed. It must be someone else!'

The farmers, great men in their own eyes, who had mainly caused Gunnar's death, ran out in their nightshifts, their shirts and breeches over their arms. 'We must get those sheep off the roof,' bawled practical Starkad. 'A new roof will cost us a fortune, the price straw is at present!'

Worrying about the money, he looked up and saw Skarp-Hedin grinning down at him. His heart stopped beating; he almost fell to the ground. He swung round and made to go back through the kitchen door, but Skarp-Hedin had dropped down beside him.

'Hey,' said Skarp-Hedin, 'don't you reckon to talk to a friend when you meet him after dark?'

Starkad dropped his breeches and backed against the farmhouse wall gasping. His heart was bumping so hard, he could not breathe. He wished he had his sword, in a way; but in another way, he knew it was no use. Skarp-Hedin crowded him in until he was hard against the wallstones; then Skarp-Hedin hefted his sword up and hit him, and Starkad slithered down the wall screaming and then died.

And Hogni with the halberd did as well. He saw Thorgeir, Starkad's son, the loud-mouthed youth who once had a fighting stallion, and came at him sweeping the halberd like a man in the hayfields with a scythe. Thorgeir yelled for pity, but Hogni still came on, feeling just one bump and no more; no more than a man in the fields feels when his scythe catches a bramble hidden deep in the corn.

'Hey,' shouted Skarp-Hedin, looking along his blade-edge to see if he had notched it, 'what about Mord of Hof now? He helped at your father's death. He even wanted to burn him out, but Gizur forbade it. Such a man deserves correction, especially since he would never have been born if Gunnar had not freed his mother to marry elsewhere. Shall we visit him?'

'Right,' said Hogni, shouldering the heavy halberd. 'Let's be off!'

So they went.

But crafty Mord of Hof was up early and, when he saw them, knew what they had come for. There was no mistake about that.

Skarp-Hedin by this time was, to tell the truth, a little weary, having lost a night's sleep; so he did not put it to Mord as quickly as he might have done earlier. Indeed, he gave that sly man time to get on to his knees and talk a while, as well as Mord could, which was not well, considering all things.

Mord gibbered away, while Skarp-Hedin was yawning before the end-knock. And only one thing he said stopped Skarp-Hedin from bringing down the blade.

'For the love of Odin,' gasped Mord, on his knees, 'I beg mercy and will offer you *full compensation for Gunnar, though he was an outlaw.*'

Hogni came up, picking his teeth, pale-faced and careless.

'What is this about outlaws?' he asked. 'Did someone speak?'

Mord beat his hands on his head. 'Oh, listen to me,' he said. 'I beg you, listen. I meant no wrong to Gunnar. I only did what the others made me do. I swear it. After all, Gunnar was good to my mother, I know. Look, I will pay out of my own pocket everything that should be paid for a man's death. I can't do more than that.'

Hogni swished the halberd through the pale dawn air a time or two, as though considering. It made a whistling sound, like silk being ripped. Mord almost went out of his mind to hear it. He buried his face in the grass.

Then Hogni said dully, 'All right, Skarp-Hedin, let him get up. We have killed four tonight, and it is almost breakfast time. This coward can pay up for all the rest— and, later on, if we feel like it, we can always come back and get him. We know where he lives.'

So Mord the Liar paid up for Gunnar's death, although Gunnar had been an outlaw. And the matter was left at that; Njal saw how the land lay, and knew that any interference would only bring on feud after feud, just as the strands of a spider's web are led, one from another, until they make a whole world in themselves.

The best thing, Njal thought, was to let the affair rest there; so as soon as he could, he married Hogni off to the pretty daughter of an Icelandic poet, and so got him busy with household affairs. After that, Hogni was too occupied with his wife and his father-in-law to go out night-killing any more.

And that is how brave Gunnar was avenged; by two youths who had seen a ghost in the moonlight and felt that they must do something about it.

11. The Insult

Now another thread must be fed into the loom, as is the way with life, which is never content with one story if it can have two for the same price.

As all will remember, Njal's sons, Grim and Helgi were faring abroad with Thrain Sigfusson, up and down the islands, in and out of the Baltic, feasting here, fighting there, and making great names for themselves among the vikings and baresarks of the Northland.

Indeed, no Icelanders were ever more welcome than they, until Thrain Sigfusson stupidly took on board a murderer and temple-spoiler, named Hrapp, whom Earl Hakon of Norway was chasing to bring to justice. Thrain got clear of harbour and set sail for Iceland, but Njal's two sons were caught by the angry Earl and would have been severely punished had it not been for the help of an Orkney viking named Kari, who made peace for them with the great Earl of Norway.

So it was that when Njal's sons returned home to Iceland at last, they still bore a grudge against Thrain Sigfusson; and so it was that Njal, grateful for the help his sons had received in their danger abroad, adopted the Orkneyman, Kari, into his own family and married him to his daughter Helga.

The steading of Bergthorsknoll now had another mouth to feed, but this Kari was worth every spoonful of porridge and every plate of meat set before him. He was such another

93

man as Skarp-Hedin, a hard-faced blow-swapper, as nimble as an ape, and one who never forgot a friend or forgave an injury. If Njal had to welcome another son into his brood of young eagles, then this Kari of Orkney was the best man he could have chosen.

In fact, Kari had as good a nose for sniffing out vengeance as fierce Gunnar himself, and that is saying something. No hound was ever keener on the scent, and this is how Kari gained his fame in the world. In all the Northland, no man ever followed his enemies, through dark and light, winter and summer, rain and shine, sickness and health, as Kari of Orkney did; and this is now the tale of how he came to be such a hunter.

At this time, all Icelanders considered themselves as free men, to come and go as they chose, to act as they thought best, and to be beholden to no man if they could help it. As far as their tempers and caution would allow, they obeyed the ruling of the Althing, for they prided themselves on their law and on the republic which they had made for themselves, away from all other kings and countries.

One of the things they most desired was not to be in debt, nor to allow any man to be in debt to them.

And now Njal's sons and Kari considered that Thrain Sigfusson, who had left them in the lurch in Norway, was much in their debt, and should be reminded of it. Also, they bore no liking for Killer-Hrapp, the man Thrain had rescued from Earl Hakon's judgement, especially since this Hrapp now had a farmstead near Thrain and was doing well in that part of Iceland, though he did not deserve to.

Many was the time when Njal's sons and Kari put

their heads together round the hearth fire at night, wondering how they might bring it home to Thrain that he had betrayed them in a way no decent Icelander should have done, when voyaging abroad among strangers.

They even sent Kari to talk to Thrain, asking him what compensation he thought of making for his bad behaviour; but Kari came back with a stern face and a hangdog look, which was not like him, and when Skarp-Hedin questioned him, he said that Thrain had spoken such words to him as could not decently be repeated. When Skarp-Hedin heard this answer, he trembled so much that he almost fell into the fire with temper.

The other brothers said nothing, but just watched him. When Bergthora, his mother, ran in with a bowl of broth to warm him, thinking her son had a chill, Skarp-Hedin knocked it aside and said between his clenched teeth, 'It will take more than a bowl of broth to cure this, Mother.'

The old woman said, 'I do not know what you are on with, you foolish fellow; all I know is that you have spilled this good mutton broth.'

Skarp-Hedin glowered at her and said, 'Soon I shall spill something else, and not from a clay bowl, Mother.'

Bergthora now had some inkling of what lay in her son's mind, so instead of scolding him further, she just got a cloth and tidied up the mess. She even smiled, and said, 'Well, I must say you look a merry band of vikings, all sitting round the hearth-stone with your brows knit and your fists clenched. Is this the way to pass a gay evening? Ah, young men have changed a deal since the old days. Now why don't you be like Thrain Sigfusson? He always has fifteen stout men in his hall, drinking and laughing.

And when *he* rides out over the hills, eight of them always go with him, to make merry. I have noticed that you boys skulk about as though you were searching for something you had lost in the grass, and dressed in your old clothes like beggar-men. But Thrain wears his gilded helmet and blue cloak, for all men to notice him, and carries shield, sword and spear, for all the world as though he is on his way to visit Father Odin himself.'

Skarp-Hedin looked up under his eyelids from his stool and said grimly, 'He may well do just that before the week is out. He does well to go prepared.'

When Bergthora had heard this, she went away quietly and got on with her tasks in the dairy, smiling to think of the brood of young eagles that nested at Njal's steading.

The young warriors now thought of what she had said, and they counted the great fighters who lived with Thrain; they were Killer-Hrapp, Gunnar Lambason, Lambi Sigurdarson, Grani Gunnarsson, Lodin and his brother, Tjorvi, among others. But this band in no way bothered the young men about the hearth fire, and at last Skarp-Hedin looked up and said, 'Very well, tomorrow we ride over to Thrain's steading and see what he has to say on the matter.' They all agreed, then went to bed; but none of them slept very well.

When they reached Thrain's farmhouse, they saw that the broad porch was crowded with warriors, and Thrain stood in their midst.

Njal's sons dismounted as though they were honoured guests and walked across the yard smiling. Then, standing before the porch, they waited for Thrain to bid them welcome in the customary Icelandic manner. But all the men stood silent and glaring, and no man spoke the welcome.

It only took Skarp-Hedin a moment to see how the land lay. So then he spoke up and said lightly, 'Well, I can see that we are all welcome here. I thank you, Thrain, for coming out to greet us in such a number.'

Wicked Hallgerd, who stood in the porch among the men, could bear this no longer and shouted out, 'I heard no one welcome you. Get out!'

Skarp-Hedin pretended to be short-sighted and peered before him in a comic way. 'I could have sworn I heard someone speak,' he said. 'Well, we can all be mistaken. It must have been some slut or outcast hag chattering in the kitchens.'

Hallgerd screamed, 'You will pay for those words, Skarp-Hedin Njal's son.'

Skarp-Hedin began to poke in his ear with his finger, as though he could not hear very well. Then he said, 'Well, Thrain, we have all come to see what compensation you mean to pay for your behaviour in Norway. As you must know, it is our Icelandic rule for vikings to stick together at all times.'

Thrain stepped forward and said mockingly, 'I never thought to see Njal's sons come like beggars to my door. This is a surprise!'

Killer-Hrapp stood beside him and said, 'Don't waste your words on such mangy dogs, Thrain. Let me deal with them, I have my axe.'

Helgi Njal's son then said, 'Yes, deal with us, fellow, and you will get no bargain out of it.'

Hrapp spluttered and began to move forward, threatening.

Skarp-Hedin said calmly, 'Aye, come on, my lad; we'll soon change that grey skin of yours to a red one. We'll stop your gallop!'

Hrapp stayed where he was then, for killer as he was, he knew when he had met his match, and big Skarp-Hedin had grown to be any man's match. His shoulders would have been as high as Gunnar's, if that man had lived.

There was a hard silence for a while, then Hallgerd screeched again, 'Go home "Little Dungbeards" and tell your doddering father, "Old Beardless", we sent you packing.'

Njal's sons and Kari now stood white-faced at this insult. At last Skarp-Hedin said, 'Do you all give us those nicknames, then?'

Everyone nodded, except Thrain, who felt that the situation was getting out of hand. But he was only one among many, and was not noticed, though he was the householder.

Then Skarp-Hedin said, 'Ah well, it is every man's right to call down on himself the fate he wishes. You have chosen yours today, following the chattering of that magpie-woman. I shall say no more on this occasion; but more will be said, though not with words, perhaps.'

Then Njal's sons and Kari went strolling back to their horses and rode away.

The men in the porch laughed after them, but their laughter had a thin sound and Thrain did not join in it.

When his sons told Njal of the insult, his first question was: 'Did you name any witnesses who would swear to those words before the Althing?'

Skarp-Hedin shook his head and said, 'I need no witnesses, Father. This affair will never reach the courts, I promise you.'

Fierce old Bergthora smiled to herself, hearing her son speak so, for now she knew that her brood of eagles were already circling over their prey.

12. Down by the River

But Thrain was no bleating lamb to be snatched up from the fields, no harmless hare in the corn, no timid squawking grouse to be plucked out of the heather. Though, to be sure, his voice was often heard up and down the villages, and seldom did it speak any good of Njal and his family, as he rode about with his fierce-eyed bodyguard. He even let his movements be known to wandering beggar-women, who lost no time in passing on the news to the folk at Bergthorsknoll.

Then, just before dawn one day, Njal woke suddenly from his sleep at the sound of an axe bumping against the wooden wall. He got up in haste and went out into the yard; and there he saw what he had half-expected to see, since he had heard such bumpings before.

His sons and Kari were outside, with Skarp-Hedin in the lead, fully armed and dressed in such bright colours that it seemed they were setting forth to a feast. Skarp-Hedin wore his blue cloak, carried a round shield, and had his great axe hoisted over his shoulder. Kari stood next to him, laughing, and waving his shield, which had a lion painted on it, about his head. He looked for all the world like a king, in his silken cloak and gilded helmet. Indeed, so did Helgi, whose red tunic matched his red shield with a hart painted on it, and whose helmet glittered in the first rays of the sun. But old Njal had seen too many young men setting out on bloody business to be deceived by fine clothes.

'And where do you think you are off to?' he called out to them.

Skarp-Hedin glanced back and said, 'Oh, looking for sheep as usual, Father.'

Njal gave him a narrow look and said, 'You told me that once before, when you were out after other animals.'

Skarp-Hedin laughed lightly in the dawn sunlight and said, 'Why, you are not as simple as you look, old Father.'

At that, Njal turned away and went back into the kitchen. By now he had come to learn that Skarp-Hedin was too old and too stubborn to be ruled by words of caution, however wise they might be. There was nothing Njal could do, and he knew it.

It was a clear, sunlit morning as the band of brothers went over the hills and sat down to wait where Thrain and his men would pass. Over their heads a lark sang, and high above the lark a hawk fluttered, waiting also.

Kari said, 'I wonder if the lark knows what is waiting for him?'

Helgi said wryly, 'I wonder if anyone does, except Njal? For all we know, we may be the lark and not the hawk.'

Skarp-Hedin grunted and said, 'Huh, do you think so, little brother?' He looked like a lion, lounging in the sun, with his tawny mane over his shoulders and his thick arms all covered with hair. In his big hands, the great axe looked like a toy. 'Huh, do you think so?' he said again and yawned.

Then Kari said hurriedly, 'Look, here they come—Thrain and his riders, spurring over the hills. By Odin, they must have seen the sunlight flashing on our shields, for they are turning to go down along the river, where we can't take them unawares.'

Skarp-Hedin yawned again and stretched, just as brave
Gunnar used to do, and said, 'Right, then let us run down
and meet them there. We are not cripples, are we? No, I
see we all have the right number of legs!'

But as he started off, the leather thong of his shoe
snapped, and he had to stop and mend it. 'Go on, brothers,'
he called, 'I will catch you up, if I can get this tied.'

Down there by the river, a broad hump of ice lay, and
here Thrain and his eight men halted in a group, to get
ready for the fight. Thrain was just fitting his helmet on
snugly when he heard a great shout and looked up to see
Skarp-Hedin coming as swift as the wind down the hill-
slope. Thrain's cold fingers had scarcely fastened the helmet-
strap when Skarp-Hedin had leaped on to the ice-hump
and was sliding down at him faster than any hawk can
swoop.

There was no time to do anything; that axe came
swinging down before Skarp-Hedin had stopped slither-
ing. He did not even pause to take aim. The blade did not
pause, either, until it had split Thrain's head to the jaws.
His back teeth spilled out on to the ice, and then Skarp-
Hedin had flashed past. Tjorvi flung his shield in the
warrior's path, but Skarp-Hedin laughed and jumped
right over it without a second thought, like a gull flying
over a rock on the seashore.

Just then the other brothers came panting on to the
scene.

'Hoho!' laughed Kari, 'but that was man's work,
brother!'

Skarp-Hedin slowed down and laughed back, 'Aye, and
now it's your turn, you lazy rogue!'

Like hounds about a stag, the brothers closed in. Loud-mouthed Hrapp came to meet them, and then staggered back, short of an arm. Helgi's axe took that off for him. Hrapp said, 'Well, well! That arm has killed a few in its time; perhaps it needed pruning, it was getting old and craggy!'

'And so do you,' said Grim, as he ran his spear through the murderer's body.

They all did brisk work, down there by the river. Kari killed Tjorvi, and Skarp-Hedin seized hold of Gunnar Lambason and Grani Gunnarsson, lifting them off their feet. 'Hey,' he called out, 'I have found a couple of puppies here. What shall I do with them?'

Helgi, who was busy at the time, shouted back, 'Finish them both, or you may live to be sorry.'

But Skarp-Hedin was in a merry mood now, and after giving them a good shaking, he said, 'Oh, dogs like this will never frighten me.'

So he flung them aside, and laughed to see them lying, wide-eyed with fear, on the wet grass. He also spared Lambi Sigurdarson and Lodin. They never forgave him for this mercy.

Then the brothers rested from their morning's work, leaning on their axe-shafts and panting, wiping their damp hair from their faces and laughing.

'Come on, lads,' said Skarp-Hedin, 'we've done enough for one day. Let's be off back to tell old Njal what the weather is like down by the river.'

And when they told Njal all that had happened, he frowned and said, 'I do not consider this a joke, sons. To me it is a serious affair, and one of you will lie stark for this morning's game.'

Skarp-Hedin slapped his father on the back. 'Oh, stop

your croaking, Father,' he said. 'You are getting as bad as an old crow.'

Then they went into the hall and ate the good breakfast Bergthora had got ready for them. She smiled to see them eat up every scrap, like wolves tearing meat.

13. The New Chieftain

IT was good to be young and strong in old Iceland; good to wear a silken coat and own a helmet and a keen axe. To live in a warm farmstead with a band of fierce brothers behind you always, was like being a king or a god. Let thunder growl; you were louder than it. Let the winds blow, you were swifter than they. Let the water freeze, you were harder than ice. Let the wolves ravage, you were fiercer than they. You were a man, a warrior, a viking; none was your master, until one day sword spat out at you, or axe fell on you, or spear ran through you, and then your day was done. Yet you never knew, if it was a clean kill, and so you went into the darkness still laughing.

Around and about the grey island, there was hardly a spot where blood had not flowed into the grass. Every hill could tell its dark tale; every river-ford its story of sword-clash and shouting. There were men in Iceland then, but such men that the old chiefs and the law-makers often shook their white heads and said, 'We cannot last much longer, for we are destroying ourselves with our bravery. We cannot breed men fast enough to make good the losses we suffer each year from feuds and ambushes and blood-atonements.'

Then God sent the answer, for a new faith was stirring in the Northland. Old Earl Hakon of Norway was now in his grave, and a new king, Olaf Tryggvason, sat in the the throne chair and ruled the land. This Olaf brought

Christianity to Norway, and spread it as far away as Shetland, Orkney and the Faroe Islands, so that all his people should be of one faith.

And soon Olaf sent out his missionary, Thangbrand, to convert the fierce Icelanders also. Oh, it was no slight task that Olaf gave this man! At first, no one would even trade with him, and he went short of food. Icelandic witches cast their spells on him; fierce baresarks tried to break up his meetings; in fact, all that could be done to hinder him was done. But this Thangbrand was no easy man to hinder; more than once he snatched up his cross and brained the heathen warriors who had come to frighten him; more than once he had matched his Christian prayers against the spells of wizards. And, in the end, the chiefs and law-givers of Iceland smiled and said, 'This Thangbrand is a sign from the Christian god. If we all follow his teachings and let ourselves be baptized, then peace will come to our suffering land, and an end will be put to feuding and murder.'

So, after much argument, they let Thangbrand baptise them, sometimes going in whole families to be received into the Christian faith. Foremost among the chiefs, as might be expected, was Njal the Wise, who set a good example to the other heathen chiefs and so led them away from Odin and Thor towards the White Christ.

Njal did even more; to make amends for the murder of Thrain, down by the river, Njal adopted Hoskuld, Thrain's son, meaning to tend him and care for him as though he had been born at Bergthorsknoll itself.

But first, Njal had to be satisfied about a certain thing, in case misunderstandings arose later. Taking the youth aside, he asked him gently, 'Will you accept this gold ring from me, Hoskuld?'

The young man nodded, smiling, and answered, 'Aye, that I will.' And when he had put the ring on, Njal said, 'Now tell me, do you know how your father met his death, my boy?'

Hoskuld nodded again and said softly, 'Yes, Njal. Skarp-Hedin killed my father, but compensation has been paid, and now there is no sense in letting the future be spoiled by the past. All is over and done with, Njal.'

Njal put his arms about the youth and said, 'I forsee a great life before you, Hoskuld. You will grow to be a great and wise chief. I ask you, will you accept me as your foster-father, Hoskuld, so that there shall be peace between our families for ever?'

Hoskuld bowed his head and replied, 'With all my heart, Njal. Let there be peace between us always, from this time on.'

So Hoskuld went home with Njal, and became a member of his family. Njal's sons soon loved this new brother of theirs, for he was not only handsome and quietly-spoken, he was very skilled in the use of all weapons. It would have been hard to find a more pleasant young man, for Hoskuld never spoke ill of anyone, and before long he was welcome at every steading in Iceland, which is saying a great deal.

The day came when Njal felt that Hoskuld had better settle down and marry a good wife, so he chose for his foster-son a high-spirited and pretty girl called Hildigunn. Njal knew that the girl was a very neat and capable needle-woman and a good cook; he also knew that she was as brave as a woman could be. These were great qualities in any wife, the way life was lived in Iceland in those days.

But what Njal did not know was that Hildigunn was, beneath her prettiness and smiles and needle-skill, harsh-natured and ruthless. In this, she was just like her uncle, the great warrior-chieftain, Flosi of Svinafell.

Njal was very wise, but even a wise man can make mistakes, and this mistake shed more blood than a battle before the tale was ended.

At first Hildigunn would not agree to marry Hoskuld unless he became a man of authority and gained a chieftainship; so Njal went to great trouble and, arguing the case at the Althing, persuaded his fellow-chieftains to set up a new Court, which was to deal with all matters that the present Quarter Courts could not settle, and over this court he arranged that Hoskuld, his foster-son, should be chief, with the new title of Hoskuld Hvitaness-Priest.

No man could have done more for Hoskuld than Njal did. He even bought some land out at Ossaby and presented it to the young people, so that they could build their home there and start life afresh.

In all ways, it looked a good match; the two families visited each other, turn and turn about, for feastings, and even stern old Bergthora praised Hildigunn as though she were the best wife a young man could have.

But all good things come to an end. One day Njal's own son, Hoskuld, who lived with his mother Hrodny at Holt, was treacherously killed by a kinsman of Hoskuld Hvitaness-Priest; yet so law-abiding was Njal that he forgave the murderer when his foster-son Hoskuld pleaded for him and awarded a compensation of two hundred ounces of silver for the dead man. Bergthora and Njal's other sons, especially Skarp-Hedin, disapproved of this settlement; yet, out of their love and respect for Hoskuld Hvitaness-Priest, they took no further action.

In fact, Skarp-Hedin that year made his foster-brother

Hoskuld a present of a four-year-old black stallion with two mares to keep him company. Quarrelling was the farthest thing from this fierce man's mind at the time.

But a quarrel had to come before long—for life was getting to be too peaceful in Iceland now that all were Christians.

Mord of Hof envied all other men, and itched like Satan to sow the seeds of ill-feeling among those who lived contented. He was the traitor who had tried to burn Gunnar in his steading, and who had begged mercy on his knees that morning when Skarp-Hedin went hunting. He had never forgiven Skarp-Hedin for shaming him so. Now Mord whispered to Hoskuld that the stallion was a worthless beast and that Skarp-Hedin had given it to him in contempt. Then he went to Njal's sons and whispered to them that, if they had only known it, Hoskuld had belittled them at their last visit by making them sleep in an outhouse. His only wish was to stir up trouble. He was more an adder than a man. His strange mind was full of flames and burnings.

'In fact,' he went on, 'I can tell you worse. The night you slept in that shed, Hoskuld, your own foster-brother, planned to burn you alive. I can assure you, he had faggots piled all round it, and he would have set light to them, save that another visitor arrived just as he was going out with the torch. Now what do you think of that?'

Little by little, Mord of Hof poisoned the minds of the two families until, at last, Njal's sons always looked suspiciously at Hoskuld whenever they met. As for Hoskuld, he was so worried that he told all to Flosi, his wife's fierce uncle, who had never really approved of the friendship between Hoskuld and Njal.

'Worry no longer,' said Flosi. 'I will see that you are protected from this Skarp-Hedin and his fierce brothers.'

Hoskuld was still a young man and did not know much of the world. When Flosi presented him with a scarlet cloak, trimmed with rich lace down the front, Hoskuld felt certain that at last he had found a true friend, and one who would stand beside him in all misfortunes.

Then this back-biting was forgotten, for spring came early to Iceland that year, and so all thrifty farmers had to be out in the fields, sowing their corn and not brooding by the fire over any tittle-tattle that blew their way like draught under a door.

14. The Early Sowing

It turned out to be the reddest sowing Iceland had known since Christianity came there, for one bright morning Mord of Hof rode in to Bergthorsknoll and, taking Njal's sons aside, told them in rapid words that Hoskuld was up to his old tricks and was plotting to get rid of them before the harvest would be reaped.

Skarp-Hedin listened coldly for a time, then said, 'Very well, friend Mord, if you are so sure of this, then we will take action against him—provided that you come with us and take part in the punishment just as we do. Now, how does that suit you, dear friend?'

Mord hadn't bargained for this turn in events, but he put a good face on it and said, 'Certainly, Skarp-Hedin. When a man knows he is in the right, he is always prepared to back up his word with deeds.'

'Good,' said Skarp-Hedin, nodding and smiling strangely. 'We will go straightway. Let everyone bring his weapons with him.'

Now, that fine morning, with the sun already shining, Hoskuld Hvitaness-Priest was up early to see to the sowing. He was wearing the scarlet cloak that Flosi had given him and had a seed-basket in one hand and a sword in the other. But, to tell the truth, his mind was on sowing corn and not swinging swords.

So, when Skarp-Hedin suddenly jumped up from behind a fence, Hoskuld started with shock, and backed away.

Skarp-Hedin called out calmly, 'No, Hvitaness-Priest, don't bother to run away, we can catch you, you scheming dog!'

Then he struck down hard at Hoskuld's head. The frightened youth let fall his sword and seed-basket as he sank to his knees.

'May God help me and forgive you all,' he said, the blood leaving him in a rush and running into the furrows.

The brothers laughed at this, and all stood round him, giving him a blow each, as they had arranged on the way. Even Mord of Hof gave his blow, though he shut his eyes when it landed. They waited until Hoskuld lay still, then they went out of the cornfield.

Mord went up to Skarp-Hedin, shivering a little, and said, 'Now I have another idea, friend.'

Skarp-Hedin looked down at him with a twitching mouth. 'Oh,' he said. 'And what is it this time? You always seem full of ideas.'

Mord could hardly get the words out. 'Look,' he said at last, 'I will go home alone, as though I had not been with you at this affair. Better still, I will say that I was just passing by Hoskuld's field and saw it all happen, powerless to prevent it. Yes, and I'll say how horrified I was, Skarp-Hedin. So, Hoskuld's kinsmen will ask me to give notice of the killing at the Althing; then I can do it in such a way that it would be illegal of the kinsfolk to take any action against you. How is that, Skarp-Hedin?'

The big man shrugged his shoulders and turned away. 'Yes, that would be fine, little man,' he said in a chill voice. 'Do that. Go away and do as you please. Whatever you do will suit me.'

Mord was only too glad to go from that place, and away

from such men, who walked with death in their wide eyes.

So Njal's sons and Kari went homewards silently, none of them talking to the others. Deep in their hearts, they had not really wished to kill Hoskuld, their foster-brother; but had only wanted to teach him a sharp lesson. But it was as though something had entered into them as they saw him fall to his knees and call on God, as though not they had struck the blows but someone else, something else, among the red furrows and the corn-seed splashed all scarlet. No killing had ever affected them so, and none of them had any stomach now for the breakfast Bergthora would have ready for them.

At the yard-gate the brothers halted. Kari said, 'Go on, Skarp-Hedin, it is your place to break the news to Njal.'

Skarp-Hedin's hands were now shaking and his legs were almost too feeble to bear his great body up. 'I wish to God another could do it for me,' he said. 'But it is my place, as you say, and I must do it.'

When old Njal had heard what they had done, he sank down on to his stool by the fire and put his hands to his tired eyes.

At last he said in a weak voice, 'You are too much for me to manage, my sons. You are beyond all my guidance now. This is the most terrible news any man has ever brought to me. It strikes so deeply down into my heart that I would willingly have lost any two of you, and still have dear Hoskuld alive in my house.'

Skarp-Hedin kicked at the stools and put on a hard face, though his own heart was brimming with grief. 'Ah,' he said, in a scornful voice, 'no wonder you are sad; you are getting to be an old fellow now, Father, and you old ones always feel such slight things keenly.'

Njal looked his son in the eye and said in a measured voice, 'If you could see as clearly as I can, young one, you too would grieve. For what you have done this morning will bring about my death, your mother's death, and your own deaths. Yes, all of my sons will die.'

Kari stepped forward and asked boldly, 'Father Njal, am I counted among your sons in this fortune-telling?'

Njal looked away and smiled sadly. 'Nay, Kari,' he said. 'There is another fate for you. It seems to me that you will be more than a match for any of your enemies, for you have the lines of good luck in your face.'

Njal's sons drew back from the old man then and went silently from the room. From that day, the thought of Hoskuld's death never left Njal's mind, and a heavy sadness always hung over him. From that day, Njal truly became an old man in all his thoughts, and speech, and movements.

15. Judgement on the Brothers

THE morning that Hoskuld died in the cornfield, his wife
Hildigunn had a bad dream and woke in terror to find that
her husband had left the bed. She dressed in haste and
hurried to the field; but she need not have hurried, for
he was still there. He would still be there by night.

Weeping, she cradled his ruined head in her lap and
sat among the furrows. 'Oh, my love, and who has done
this thing to you?' she wailed.

Just then, Liar-Mord's shepherd came past and called
over the fence, 'Why, lady, Skarp-Hedin did it. Do you
need to ask? And all the sons of Njal were in it too; they
galloped past me like black-faced trolls not an hour
since.'

Hildigunn gritted her white teeth and said to herself,
'This would have been a real man's work—if only one
man had done it; but since many had a hand in it, it is
cowardly murder and they shall pay dearly for it.'

Then she stripped her husband of the scarlet cloak that
Flosi had given him and with it she wiped away all the
blood from him, so that the scarlet was soon clotted with
a deeper dye.

'I will see this cloak is put to work,' she said, putting
the sodden rag into her dower-chest.

Meanwhile, Liar-Mord had spread the news of the killing,
and then rode back to the cornfield with many witnesses;
there, standing over the body, he pointed out each wound,

and said who had given it. Naturally, he did not mention the wound he himself had made.

After that, the black news spread like heath-fire across Iceland and soon all the farmers and fishermen were talking of it, recalling what a pleasant man poor Hoskuld had been, and saying that Njal's sons had at last over-reached themselves and must suffer, as a pack of savage wolves would have to suffer. Never had Iceland been so furious at one man's killing.

As for Flosi, he was angry enough, but when he called on Hildigunn and she suddenly drew the red-drenched cloak from her dower-chest and wrapped it round him, charging him to avenge Hoskuld in blood, he was both furious and horrified. For a moment, he forgot himself and called her a monster, a ruthless witch, and so on; then he repeated the old saying, that the counsels of women have always been cold since the world began.

But when he had regained his composure, Flosi told the bereaved widow that he would do all in his power to bring the killers to justice at the summer Althing, which was soon about to open.

There were very few men in Iceland who had a good word to say for Skarp-Hedin and his brothers now. Certain envious men demanded both outlawry and blood-vengeance against them; but not even Flosi would go as far as that.

'You can either send a man away for life,' he argued among his neighbours, 'or you can kill him—but it stands to reason that you can't do both, not even to Skarp-Hedin, though he seems to deserve it!'

In fact, furious as Flosi had been at first, even he now realised that there was a limit to the punishment which the Althing might award to the killers. For, in cases like this, if

the punishment were too severe, then in years to come men
would look on the Njal family as martyrs, and other
blood-feuds would start to avenge them.

As for Skarp-Hedin, if he felt any remorse now he did
not show it. Instead, he prepared for the Althing by dressing
in his very best clothes. He wore a blue tunic with a silver
belt, blue-striped trousers, and black boots that reached
to the knee. His hair was well combed and drawn back
sleekly. He kept it in place with a headband of silk. On
his arm he carried his round shield, and over his right
shoulder he bore his axe, 'Battle-Troll', the weapon with
which he had split Thrain's skull and spilled his teeth on
the ice that day.

Anyone seeing him, even for the first time, would have
known straightway who he was. Not since great Gunnar's
time had there been such another warrior in the north.

Old Njal watched his son getting ready so gaily and
said, 'Well, Skarp-Hedin, and what plans have you and
your bold brothers in mind now?'

Skarp-Hedin glanced casually at his father and said,
'We are not as fortunate as you, old man; we have no
dreams and visions to guide us! So we shall just ride down
to the court and see what happens.'

He spoke as though it was like a feast, and not as though
that day his life might be at stake if the court judged against
him.

As he went through the door he half-turned and said,
as though he did not care, 'And you, Father? Were you
thinking of looking in at the Althing by any chance?'

Njal, who was one of the greatest lawyers Iceland had
ever known, and whose advice was always being asked in
court, nodded and said gravely, 'I shall be there, son. I

shall stand by you always, while I am alive. And perhaps, today, there may be judges present who will be lenient towards you because of the fondness and respect they have for me, old as I am.'

Skarp-Hedin went away laughing among the brothers, and Njal followed some time later, dressed soberly in his blue cloak and felt hood, and carrying a small axe in his hand. He was so weary now, it was hard work riding, and when he reached the great meadow where the court was held he had to be lifted from the saddle, his limbs were so stiff.

As for his sons and Kari, they soon scented among the crowds that they were unpopular and that, if the affair came to blows, they would be greatly outnumbered by those who now disliked them.

So it struck them as a good plan to go from booth to booth, where the great chieftains rested, to see what backing they could count on. Skarp-Hedin did not deign to ask for help, but just stood in the doorways with his axe over his shoulder, smiling in his grim way. Most of the chiefs admired this tall manly warrior with his chestnut hair and his pale face, but they lost no time in telling him that he always brought bad luck to any who had dealings with him. In most of the booths Skarp-Hedin then let his sharp tongue run away with him and offended the chiefs; so that in the end the brothers had few men to support their case. But that was his nature and he could not help himself; Skarp-Hedin was his own worst enemy and always he would rather lose a friend than grovel for help.

That Friday evening the court sat and Njal obtained the services of Thorhall as his lawyer. Now this Thorhall was Njal's foster-son and had learned his profession from

Njal himself, so coming to be one of the best advocates in Iceland. It was not long before he sniffed out, from rumours here and there, that Liar-Mord of Hof himself had struck a blow at Hoskuld but had never mentioned this when he was showing the wounds to the witnesses. It was obvious, then, that by suppressing evidence, Mord had put himself in the wrong and that no suit brought by him would be valid. What is more, by holding the law in such contempt Mord was himself liable to outlawry.

All this Thorhall made plain in his speech before the court, ending by telling Flosi that the whole case was invalidated and that Njal's sons and Kari could not now be judged.

For a while there was such heavy silence in the meadow that it seemed as though a thunder-clap might sound at any moment and that fighting would surely break out.

But old Njal stood up and said, 'I beg you all to listen to me. I loved Hoskuld more dearly than my own sons. When I learned that he had been killed, it was as if the sweetest light of my eyes had been extinguished. I would rather have lost all my sons and have Hoskuld still alive. So, I beg you, although Thorhall has proved to you that this suit is invalid, let the greatest chiefs among you name a compensation-price for his death, and I promise you, however high that price is, it will be paid here and now.'

Even Flosi had to agree that these words were just and reasonable. And so it was that the court imposed the highest sum ever known in Iceland for a man-killing. It was six hundred ounces of silver. There was some difficulty in raising it immediately, but in the end this sum was brought into court and it seemed that the affair was over, sad as it had been.

But just then something happened which not even wise Thorhall could have predicted, a small thing in itself, but one which brought great consequences, as a simple tile might do, slipping from a roof and killing a passer-by.

Old Njal, seeing how generously all present had contributed to the fine, placed on the heap of silver a silk cloak and a fine pair of boots, as an extra offering to show his good will.

When Flosi stalked in to collect the money, he picked up this silken cloak and examined it scornfully. To him, it looked like a woman's cloak and so he regarded such an offering as an insult to a warrior like himself.

'Oh, and who has given this pretty garment?' he asked, staring about him, standing stiff-legged like an angry dog.

At first there was silence, for no one knew what was in this fierce man's mind.

'What!' he called out. 'Does no one dare tell me the answer to my simple question, then?'

Skarp-Hedin had been very quiet all through the hearing and the judgement, but now his hackles rose like those of a hound.

He went stiff-legged towards Flosi and said, 'Who do you think gave it?'

Flosi turned and stared above him haughtily, his nostrils flaring. 'I would guess that your father gave it,' he said. 'You know, the one we call "Old Beardless", because no man knows whether he is a man or a woman!'

Flosi expected that there would be laughter in the court at this rude joke, but silence fell again and he was left there alone with Skarp-Hedin breathing heavily beside him.

Skarp-Hedin came forward a stiff pace and said through

clenched teeth, 'You do ill to mock an old man, Chieftain. No real man has ever done that to Njal before, and you would never have dared when Njal was as young as I am, say. Now let me tell you this; old Njal is a man all right, and he is the father of men too. And those men who are Njal's sons have never had to go to court for their revenge when any of their kinsmen have been struck down. We are not like some I could name. We are not named Flosi.'

Flosi flew into a great rage now and kicked the pile of money aside, saying that he would not accept the court's judgement after such words. Instead, he asked for blood-vengeance on Njal's sons.

But the final judgement had already been given and could not be taken back simply because of this outburst. Instead, two of the judges had charge of the money until Flosi might come to his senses and take it away.

So the Althing ended; but not the feud which had been started by the silken cloak.

16. Gathering of Vultures

Up in the hills at Almanna Gorge, dark-faced war-men gathered, wearing their helmets and carrying their swords and axes. As they sat with their hair blowing in the wind, and their horses' manes swirling, they looked more like beasts of prey than men.

Flosi counted them and they were more than a hundred. He smiled to himself, and whispered, 'You will not have to wait long for your vengeance, Hoskuld. Not long now.'

Then he swung his pony out so as to face the angry warriors.

'My friends,' he called in a high voice. 'What is your wish, then?'

Gunnar Lambason spoke for all others as he shouted, 'We shall never be satisfied until every one of Njal's sons is killed.' He had never forgotten the day when Skarp-Hedin shook him like a dog.

The other warriors beat upon their shields at these words and the crows flying above the host wheeled away, squawking, afraid of this din and shouting.

Flosi smiled and cried out, 'For my part, dear friends, I will never give up this cause until one side or the other is utterly destroyed. Are you content?'

Once more the shields rattled and the shouting rose: 'We are content, Flosi! We are content!'

So the avengers took an oath, up there on the wind-swept rocks, to meet again in the autumn and then to ride down to Bergthorsknoll and put all in that steading to fire and sword.

That long summer a heavy weight hung over Njal's steading, a dark cloud, a threat of thunder, a feeling that the skies would open at any minute and let fall a shower of blood. This was in the air, in the minds of all that doom-driven household.

Kari felt it, also, but he knew that he must stay and face what might come to them. Indeed, all of them must stay, for there was no getting away from the island without being seen, even if Njal's sons had wanted to run from the gathering storm.

In all, at Bergthorsknoll, there were about thirty men able to bear arms, including thralls and carles. But those who followed Flosi outnumbered them by at least four to one.

Rumours spread quickly on any island and it was not long before Njal and his family knew something of what lay in store for them.

A strange thing happened at Njal's steading. An old woman lived there, named Saeunn; in her time she had acted as servant and nurse to all Njal's family and was treated with kindness because of her long service. Njal was specially fond of her because like himself she had certain moods during which she could see a little way into the future and could forecast what would happen. Njal's sons often told her she was nothing but an old gossip who talked too much, but all the same much of what she said came true in the end.

Now one day, old Saeunn suddenly got up from her bench and snatching a stick hobbled round the farmstead to where a stack of field-weeds lay by the wall. Then, cursing the heap and calling it a wretched traitor, she began to slash at it with the stick as though it was alive.

Skarp-Hedin was working in the yard when he heard her angry voice, so he strolled over and said, 'Now what's the matter, old woman? Has this heap of rubbish been misbehaving, then?'

The old woman turned on the laughing man and gazing at him with pale-blue eyes, said in her croaking voice, 'You may smile, young fellow, but this heap of rubbish will be used as death-kindling when they come to burn your father and mother. Take my advice and burn it yourself now, or throw it into the river.'

Skarp-Hedin lost his smile then, and said in a serious voice, 'No, old one, that would be useless. If what you say is to happen, then it would make no difference even if I got rid of this weed. There are other things lying about the farmyard that would make good kindling.'

Yet old Saeunn was not satisfied by these words and all the summer she kept nagging at the various sons to get rid of the weed. Smiling, they promised to do what she said but, somehow or other, they never did do it because other tasks kept them so busy about the farm.

When autumn came, Flosi gathered his riders secretly and, having had matins said one Sunday morning, they made their way towards Bergthorsknoll, planning to reach the farmstead by nightfall.

It was almost as though Bergthora expected something to happen that day because, as the family sat down at table, she said, 'This meal will be our last together, my children, so I want you all to choose your favourite food and to eat well of it.'

Usually Bergthora was such a thrifty housewife that she

was careful how much she set before her hungry family, so these words carried great weight especially with the brothers.

While they were telling her not to talk so foolishly, old Njal suddenly struck his fists on the table and cried out, 'It has come to me now! I see what is to happen! Look, both the gable walls are down and there is blood all over the table and the food!'

Now all the family was worried except Skarp-Hedin, who said calmly, 'Please sit still, all of you. I want to hear no weeping and wailing in this house. Remember, that whatever is to happen, our story will be told in Iceland in after-years, and we, the kin of Njal, will be judged by stricter standards than are ordinary men. This is as it should be, for I am thankful to say we are not ordinary men.'

He sat down proudly and went on with his eating, as though nothing had happened. But when that meal was over, Njal spoke again and warned them all not to go to bed that night.

So it was that the old man and his family were standing outside in the farmyard when Flosi and his band of men dismounted and walked towards the house. This was something the avengers had not expected, for Njal's household numbered about thirty men and all of them looked prepared, with one sort of weapon or another.

Flosi halted in his tracks and whispered, 'I hardly think we should come out of this unscathed if we pressed forward now, my friends.'

Skarp-Hedin the sharp-eyed noted this and said to his father, 'Hm, we have given them something to think about, old man! I suggest we stay out here, in a line before the house, and that will steady those cowardly wolves!'

But now Njal had become the master in his own family

again, and he said, 'No, son, that is not the way. I want you all inside, for this house is as strongly built as a fortress —and you remember how Gunnar held his enemies at bay by staying indoors, even though he was only one against many.'

But Skarp-Hedin would not be brushed off so easily. 'You make a mistake there, Father,' he said firmly. 'The men who attacked Gunnar were for the most part honourable warriors who scorned to take unfair advantages; but if these carrion once get us inside the house, they will have no more qualms about burning us out than I should have about setting fire to a wasp's nest. No, I don't want to be stifled, like a fox in his den, old man.'

At this, Njal flared up for the first time. 'My sons,' he said, 'this is not the first time you have ignored me recently. Yet, when you were boys, you did everything I said and in those days our family was more fortunate, if you will cast your minds back a bit.'

Helgi spoke up for Njal and said, 'Come on, brothers, let us do what Father says. He knows best, after all. He is the master.'

But Skarp-Hedin shrugged his massive shoulders and said, 'I am not so sure of that, Helgi. As you have seen, he is a doomed man anyway, and doomed men say strange things. All the same, if he wants us to burn with him inside the house, I'm willing. Death has never frightened me too much. I'll roast with the next man!'

Then he bent towards Kari, whom he loved, and whispered, 'All the same, brother, let us keep close together, you and I. We shall get on best if we are not separated.'

Kari nodded. 'That is what I had intended,' he said.

Skarp-Hedin slapped him lightly on the back. 'Good

127

man,' he said. 'And if my family is destroyed, I hope you will avenge us, just as we shall avenge you, if you meet with bad luck. Agreed?'

Kari nodded. 'Agreed, brother,' he said.

And so they went indoors, following the old man.

17. Glow in the Sky

WHEN Flosi saw the family go inside, he turned to his men and called out, 'Now they are doomed, my friends. See that you stand guard round all the doors and windows, for none of this blood-thirsty brood must escape.'

From time to time, Flosi's men tried to push in here and there, but each time fell back with wounds or death.

One stubborn warrior, Hroald Ozurarson, rushed silently at Skarp-Hedin, hoping to pin him with a spear; but that great fighter swung round on him suddenly, as though he had eyes in the back of his head, hacked the spear in two, then, with a most deft blow, not only dashed Hroald's shield against his body, but swung the back-horn of the axe up into his face, so that he fell dead instantly without a complaint.

Kari admired this pretty stroke and could not hold back from admitting it. 'Why, brother Skarp-Hedin,' he said, 'once you start, no one can escape you. I swear, you are the finest fighter I ever saw. Yes, I swear it!'

Skarp-Hedin, grinning a little with the embarrassment of this praise, said meekly, like a girl, 'Oh, I don't know.'

But Flosi knew; and when he had counted his wounded after a while, he called back his men and told them, 'Look, this is foolish. We have the great advantage in numbers, *but we are losing this fight*. Obviously, we cannot defeat these men with ordinary weapons, so we have two courses left open to us: we can either retreat, or we can set fire to the house and burn the enemy where they lurk. If we do the first, we not only lose our good name as warriors, but Njal's sons will no doubt follow us and kill us one by one. And if we do the second, it will be a most unchristian act—but, I am afraid, my friends, it is what we must steel ourselves to do, though we are baptised men, all of us.'

Flosi's band nodded sullenly, and so they kindled the heap of weed that old Saeunn had wanted to have destroyed, and with this made a great blaze in front of each door, since it was as dry as tinder after the summer's sunshine.

Skarp-Hedin looked from a window and said to them, 'Ah, I notice you are making a fire, lads. Are you thinking of doing some cooking, then?'

His enemy Grani called back, 'Aye, Skarp-Hedin, we shall soon have the blaze going fierce enough to do a bit of roasting.'

However, for a while, the women of the farmstead threw buckets of whey, from which the milk-curds had been strained, on to the fires and doused them; but at last the dry rubbish really caught, and soon the wooden ceiling of Njal's hall was flaming from end to end, being so dry after that long summer.

Njal, hearing the women-folk crying out, smiled at them and said gently, 'Now then, what is all this noise? There is no need for fear, my loves! After all, look at it this way, if you burn in this world, you can't burn in the next, for God is too merciful to allow that!'

He had hardly finished when all the house was ablaze, being largely of rushes and wood, so walking calmly to the window, Njal called out to Flosi, 'Would you consider making an agreement with my sons, Flosi, or letting anyone out of this farmstead?'

Flosi came straight to the point. 'I will come to no terms whatever with your sons, Njal. I intend to settle those vipers once and for all, and will not move an inch from here until they are all dead. But as for letting anyone out of the house, I will certainly allow the women, the children and the ordinary servants to go free without the slightest harm.'

So all the women and children began to file out into the yard. One of them, named Astrid, persuaded Njal's youngest son, Helgi, to dress as a woman and see if he could escape. Against his will and really as a joke, he did so, wearing a headscarf and a long cloak, and walking among his sisters and other relations.

But Flosi's eyes were keen, and he said, 'Hey, that's a tall and broad-shouldered woman. Seize her!'

Helgi was naturally carrying a sword beneath the cloak, and in a flash the weapon was out and swinging. It took off a man's leg before Flosi came up behind Helgi and swept away his head with one blow.

When he had wiped his sword, Flosi went to the main door and offered to let Njal and his old wife Bergthora go free from the burning farmstead.

But Njal shook his grey head and said, 'No, thank you, Flosi. I am too old now to avenge my sons, and I would not want to live on in shame, you understand, without taking any action. The bread would be bitter in my mouth.'

Flosi was now almost frantic. He called out to Berg-thora, 'Lady, I beg you to leave the farm, for I would not harm you on any account. Please leave, Bergthora, and take Njal with you.'

But the old lady only sniffed at him and said quietly, 'When I married Njal, I was very young; but even then I promised to stay with him all his days, and I see no reason for breaking my marriage vow, thank you, Flosi. You show a generous heart, for such a miserable fellow.'

Then she turned with a smile and said to her husband, 'Well, what shall we do now, old one?' It was almost as though she was on a holiday.

Njal thought a while, then said, 'Let us go to our bed and rest a little.'

And that was what they did, slowly and without concern.

Now Kari had a little son named Thord who loved Njal and Bergthora most dearly. When he saw the old couple going to bed, he ran to them and said, 'Can I come into bed with you, Grandmother?'

'Oh, no,' said Bergthora. 'You must go away with the others from the farm. We can't have you burned, my love. That would never do.'

But Thord kept crying and saying, 'That's not fair, Grandmother! You always said we should never be parted, and now you are sending me away. I won't go! I won't go!'

So in the end Bergthora took the boy in her arms and drew him into bed, laying him between herself and her husband, to be as safe as possible under the circumstances.

Njal called his bailiff over and said to him, 'I want you to take notice where we are lying, and how we have disposed ourselves, my good fellow. You will then know where to look for our remains, for we do not intend to move again now, however fierce the fire becomes.'

The man promised, weeping. Then Njal ordered him

to spread a new damp ox-hide over them all, to keep away what flying sparks it might.

After that, the old man and his wife crossed themselves and the boy, commended their souls to God, and lay back gently.

Skarp-Hedin watched all this, then turned to Kari and said, 'Father is really getting to be an old man. See how early he has gone to bed. Why, at one time he would sit up all night, as long as there was a fire to see by! How things do change, to be sure!'

For a time after this, Skarp-Hedin, Kari and Grim kept together, harassing the enemy as much as they could by flinging burning pieces of wood at them and causing many of the attackers some discomfort. Flosi saw that it was only a matter of time before the charred roof came down, and so commanded his men to take no more risks, but to withdraw to the yard and let the fire fight for them.

Suddenly, with a rending crash the main beams fell from the roof. Standing in a shower of sparks, Skarp-Hedin said, 'Well, that lot must have killed my father. He was a good old man and never coughed or groaned once throughout this fire, though the smoke must have got on his chest.'

That was his last praise for Njal the Wise and, coming from Skarp-Hedin, it was perhaps praise enough.

Now at one end of the long hall a cross-beam had lodged in falling, so that it formed a sloping ramp to the top of the wall. Kari cast his keen eye over it and said, 'Smoke is forming a screen about us, Skarp-Hedin. Let us take advantage of the moment and run up that beam on to the wall-top. With luck, we could jump down on the other side and be away.'

Skarp-Hedin nodded. 'Right,' he said. 'You go first, and I will follow.'

Kari grew impatient and answered, 'Look, there is no time to lose. Get up on the beam and be off with you. I will follow you.'

Skarp-Hedin bowed in mockery. 'After you, Kari,' he said.

Kari was really angry now and said, 'You grow more stupid every day, brother. Suppose you cannot get up the beam, with your great weight, and I am on the other side of the wall—well, I shall not feel inclined to come back again to save you, you know, much as I love you.'

Skarp-Hedin slapped him on the shoulder and laughed.

'My dear friend,' he said, 'if you escape, that will make me very happy, because then there will be still one left to avenge our family. So, off you go, Kari, and good luck go with you.'

Kari said no more, but turned as swiftly as a hare and dashed up the sloping beam, screened by smoke. On the wall-top, he snatched up a blazing piece of timber and hurled it down on to the men who stood beneath, scattering them. Then with his clothes and hair on fire, he leaped down, landed safely, and ran across the farmyard, with no one to bar his way in all the crackling and confusion.

One of the attackers rubbed his smoke-filled eyes and said, 'Hey, did I see a man jumping down from the roof just then?'

'No,' replied another, 'you are imagining things. It was only that fool Skarp-Hedin throwing brands at us. No one has got out of this house, you can take my word for that, and no one ever will now!'

But Kari was free, despite the man's words; and once

out of the stack-yard, he plunged on and on until he came to a small stream into which he flung himself to extinguish his burning clothes and hair. Then, as the black smoke drifted his way again, he ran bent double beneath it until he came to a little hollow, where he lay hidden until it was safe to go on again.

With Skarp-Hedin, things did not go so well. He was too heavy a man to scale the beam as nimble Kari had done, although he tried twice. The second time the smouldering beam cracked under him, flinging him back into the blaze.

'Well,' he said to himself, 'it is something to know what one's future is to be!'

Now the clouds of smoke were so dense that Skarp-Hedin's eyes began to water, and just then his old enemy Gunnar Lambason clambered up on to the wall and shouted down, 'What, are you crying, Skarp-Hedin?'

'No,' answered the warrior, 'though my eyes are smarting a bit in this smoke. It gets everywhere. But, tell me, am I right in thinking that you are laughing at me?'

Gunnar Lambason nodded and said, 'I certainly am. I am laughing for the first time since you killed Thrain, and that is a fair time ago.'

Skarp-Hedin began to grope in his belt-purse. 'Well,' he said, not looking at Gunnar for the moment, 'here is something to remind you of that day!'

Suddenly he turned and flung a double-tooth which he had knocked from dead Thrain's jawbone with the axe and had kept as a lucky charm all this time. The big tooth took Gunnar by surprise and struck him in the middle of the eye, blinding him, and toppling him down out of sight.

Then Skarp-Hedin went to his brother, Grim, and grasped both of his hands. 'Let us see if we can stamp the fire out, brother,' he said. 'At least, it will pass the time and we have nothing better to do.'

This they did for a while, dancing on the glowing embers like great bears, until suddenly Grim fell dead.

Now Skarp-Hedin was quite alone with only the flames licking round him. He staggered along the side wall until he reached the gable end of the house and, as he stood there, the rest of the roof fell in, pinning him so hard to the wall that even with his great strength Skarp-Hedin could not move an inch in any direction.

Outside in the farmyard Flosi and his men waited until it was broad daylight once more and the red glow of the burning farmhouse had faded from the sky to give place to the sun.

While they were still watching in case anyone was alive in that charred shell of a house, a local man called Geirmund rode up and said, 'Well, you have taken drastic action here, I must say.'

Flosi nodded almost sadly and said, 'That is what all Iceland will say; and to tell the truth, I am sorry it had to be. But there is nothing we can do about it now.'

Geirmund asked, 'How many folk of note died in the blaze, then?'

Flosi named the dead ones, but Geirmund stopped him suddenly and said, 'You needn't include Kari. I met him and spoke with him only this morning. True, his hair was burnt off and his clothes were the worse for fire, but he was alive, I assure you. In fact, my neighbour, Bard, lent him a horse to ride away on.'

When Flosi heard these words his face lost all its colour

and he stood trembling as though he had a wintry chill. At last he said, 'Tell me, had this man any weapons with him when you saw him?'

Geirmund nodded. 'Aye,' he answered, 'he had that sword of his, "Life Taker", under his arm. I noticed that one of its edges was discoloured and I told him that the metal must have got softened in the fire. But he only laughed and said that he would soon harden it again in the blood of the Burners. Those were his very words.'

When Geirmund had finished speaking, Flosi turned to his men and said, 'So, you have heard how it is to be. Our time of peace is ended, for Kari will not break his word, any more than Gunnar ever did. We can expect him to harry us from hill to hill, river to river, coast to coast, to pay us back for the burning. I advise you all to keep together, and especially you Sigfussons, sons of Thrain, for he will come looking for you without a doubt. It would be better if you left your farms and came to live with me in the east quarter of the island.'

Just then Modolf, one of the Burners, stepped forward and began to recite a poem he had made about the noble fire which avenged Hoskuld; but Flosi silenced him, ill-temperedly, and said, 'Never boast of killing old Njal; that was no great achievement for such a number as we are.' They could tell that Flosi had little stomach for what he had done, now that it was over.

Then suddenly a sound came from within the blackened shell of the farmhouse. It seemed that somewhere, among the flames that still crackled, a voice was intoning this verse:

'*Ah, a woman will find it more than she can do*

To stop the tears from falling, rain from a cloud,
When she thinks of how this battle ended,
This burning of old Njal's steading near the sea.'

The Burners stood white-faced at this, for it was Skarp-Hedin's voice that still spoke.

Grani said in astonishment, 'Is he alive or is he dead, do you think?'

Flosi answered impatiently, 'I shall not waste my time guessing.'

Then Grani said, 'Let us go in and look for him; I am curious.'

Flosi turned on his comrade in anger. 'You must be a fool,' he said, 'to make such a suggestion. Why, all over this district by now men will be gathering to ride down here and take us prisoner—or worse—for this night's work. My command is that we get away from here as fast as we can.'

Then they galloped off towards the Rang River.

One thing only asks to be said before this part of the sad story is ended; as the Burners galloped away, Flosi remembered a man named Ingjald, who had sworn to be with them that night but had not turned up. Now, in his bitter mood, he wished to punish this man for not sharing the blame of Njal's burning with the rest of them. So they spurred towards his farm at Keldur.

It was not necessary to seek far, for without warning they came on Ingjald down by the river, with the stream between him and them.

Flosi shouted out at him, reproaching him with breaking his word but offering to spare his life if he came over humbly and put himself at their mercy.

Ingjald laughed across the blue water and said, 'I would rather ask for Kari's mercy, Burner. As for your killing me, I am not afraid of you or your great band.'

This answer infuriated Flosi, for up till now no man had so disregarded his authority. So he yelled back, 'If you are not a coward, stay there and I will send you a present!'

Ingjald nodded and replied, 'Send it. I do not intend to move an inch.'

Then Flosi snatched a spear and hurled it at the man. His aim was strong and true, for the weapon not only split Ingjald's shield, it pierced his thigh and went down into the wood of his saddle.

In spite of his dark mood, Flosi laughed now and shouted, 'Did that one touch you, Ingjald?'

The man held back his groans as he quietly dragged the spear from his leg. Then he answered in a calm voice, 'Yes, it did, but I would call that a scratch, not a real wound. Now, if you are not a coward, stay still while I reply.'

He hurled the spear back over the water. It flew straight at Flosi's body. Seeing it in flight, the Chief lost his courage and reined his pony back a pace. It struck his bravest nephew, Thorstein, who sat behind him, toppling him dead from the saddle.

Then Ingjald laughed loud and, swinging his own horse round, rode off into the woods and away, ignoring the trail of blood he left behind.

Flosi gazed down at his dead nephew sadly. 'Now I know that ill-luck is on us,' he said. 'The best we can do is to ride up into Thrihyrning Mountain, where we can be safe for a time, while the hue and cry is on. From the ridge, we can look down on the land and see where men are gathering against us. What more can we do?'

And that is the miserable way the Burning ended, with Njal's family dead and the Burners scuttling away from their crime, as frightened as hares running from the corn when the reaper approaches.

Kari's Revenge

18. The News Spreads

SOON Icelanders were gathering, aghast at the Burning, to bring Flosi to justice. But though, led by Kari and Ingjald, they sniffed about like hounds, they could not find the hidden band. This angered the stern farming chiefs, especially a nephew of old Njal, named Thorgeir, who swore he would plead for the Burners' outlawry at the Althing, and afterwards press on to kill them. Other chiefs felt that they should ride off straightway and pull down the house of every Burner, as one destroys a hornet's nest.

But Mord of Hof, the liar who had first started the quarrel against Hoskuld, spoke up now, and for once what he said made good sense—though there were still those who were suspicious of him. Mord said, 'No, do not destroy their houses, for, if you let them stand, the Burners will one day return home to see their wives, then we can catch them.'

Up in the high mountain, though, Flosi's Burner-band had no intention of going back home to put their necks in a noose. Instead, they all rode secretly into the eastern district away from the scene of the crime, and at Flosi's farmstead they got ready for a siege.

It was about this time that Flosi had a disturbing dream. In it he saw a great giant, wearing a goatskin and carrying an iron staff, break out from the hillside, and call all the names of the Burners, one by one, in a loud voice. In his dream, Flosi went up to the man and asked his name.

'I am Iron-Grim,' said the giant, 'and I am on my way to the Althing, where I shall first clear the jury, then the court, and then the field for battle.'

While Flosi considered these stark words, the giant in the goatskin threw back his head and spoke a poem, in a voice like thunder:

> *'Soon a great fighter*
> *Will conquer this land.*
> *Then all the fields*
> *Will sprout with heads.*
> *The clash of sharp swords*
> *Will echo from hills.*
> *Men's limbs will stream*
> *With blood's dark dew.'*

When the poem was over, the giant struck the ground with his iron staff, making a tremendous crash; the hills opened again, and he walked inside, to be lost in the darkness.

Flosi woke up, sweating with dread, and told one of his followers about the dream. The man said gravely, 'This is serious. All the men named in that dream must be doomed to death. If I were you, Flosi, I would not mention this to anyone else, or you will knock the heart out of them.'

Flosi agreed, and as soon as Christmas was over he called his band together and said, 'Let us scour the country now for any men who will stand by us at the Althing, for I fear we shall need all the support we can get, and perhaps all the swords we can get, too.' But he told no one of his fateful dream.

Kari was no less troubled in his mind than Flosi, and after brooding for a while on the Burning, he found that he could no longer sleep at nights. By day, he was always talking about Njal and Skarp-Hedin, as though they were the only things in his mind. He even made up this poem:

> *My eyes are open*
> *All through the night,*
> *Seeing Skarp-Hedin,*
> *That proud warrior;*
> *Seeing the flames*
> *That burned wise Njal.*
> *Try as I might,*
> *Grief will not go.*

One day he went with a friend down to the burned steading at Bergthorsknoll and searched among the ruins and the deep layers of white ash. Below all, under a dried-up ox-hide, they found Njal and Bergthora and Kari's son, little Thord, lying in the bed. The old folk were quite unmarked by fire, and as for Thord, only one finger had been burned off when he had reached out his hand from under the hide. Though they were dead, they still looked as pleasant as though they were still alive. Seeing this, Kari and his friend gave praise to God for such a kind miracle. Crowds came to see the bodies and one man said, 'Njal's face and body have a radiance which I have never before seen on a dead man.' All the others agreed.

Then they set about to look for Skarp-Hedin's body. They found it pressed against the gable wall, where he had held himself upright to the end, although his legs below the knees had been burnt off. It was seen that he had

147

endured great pain, for he had bitten right through his upper lip; but his eyes, though open, were not swollen or in any way unsightly.

What best showed the sort of man he was, was his axe. This he had driven into the wall so hard that most of the blade was buried in the wood and so was not softened by fire. Only a warrior, proud of his weapons, would have done this at such a time.

Kari gave this fine axe to that Thorgeir who had sworn to carry on the blood-feud. 'You are the outstanding man of old Njal's family now,' he said, as Thorgeir took the axe reverently. 'Besides, it is so heavy that only you could wield it.'

When they examined Skarp-Hedin's body, they found two burn-marks, one on his chest and one between his broad shoulders, and both in the shape of the cross. They decided that fierce Skarp-Hedin had branded himself with these marks, bitter though it must have been, to signify at the last that he offered himself to God.

Digging here and there, the seekers also found other bodies, making eleven in all; and these they carried to church for Christian burial.

Bad news affects different people in different ways. Thorhall the Lawyer, who had learned his profession from old Njal and never ceased to proclaim his debt, was usually the most controlled of men, as is fitting in a lawyer; but when he heard the details of the Burning, blood suddenly spurted from both his ears and he fell to the earth senseless. When the flow stopped, he got up again and said, 'I am sorry about that; it was no proper way for a man to behave. However, it gives me some guidance in the course I must follow; for, from now onward, I shall seek vengeance for my blood that was shed, from those who burned Njal, my foster-father.'

Since Thorhall was so great an advocate, this was good news for Kari to hear, especially as the Althing was soon to assemble and try this case.

All the same, things did not go smoothly, for, soon after this, Thorhall developed a poisonous boil on his foot which caused his leg to swell so big and red that he could hardly think of law, much less walk about in courts, as a lawyer often has to do when persuading the jury to agree with him.

However, Kari and his many friends pressed on gathering supporters, and by threatening Liar-Mord, they forced him to start the law-case against Flosi and the Burners. This much must be said for Mord, once he had now given his oath, he stuck to his word, naming witnesses and calling inquests on the recovered bodies. Mord was able to do this, in law, on the grounds that Njal's only surviving kinsman, Thorgeir, had appointed him to lead the law-suit.

As for Flosi, when he rode to the Althing with a hundred and twenty followers, it crossed his mind to make a last defiant gesture before the court assembled; so he went to the farmstead of Thorhall's father, Asgrim, hoping to humble him, and so cause him to dissuade his lawyer-son from pressing the case too hard against the Burners.

Asgrim sensed what was in Flosi's mind even before the riders dismounted in the stack-yard; but he was clever enough not to let these fierce men see that he understood, in case they murdered him too.

So he bustled the servants round, made them decorate the feast-hall, and lay a generous meal; though when

Flosi swaggered in, Asgrim gave him no greeting but merely pointed to the food. In this way, Asgrim could not later be accused of violating the Icelandic laws of hospitality, by welcoming a guest and then trying to get him killed. Such rules were most strictly observed in the northern world at this time.

However, as the feasting went on, and Asgrim saw that Flosi was guarded by four men with axes, the old man grew more and more angry to think that his boastful enemy sat at his table, eating his meat and drinking his ale, as though he could get away with anything. Then, when mounting fury could not be held in any longer, the old man jumped up and, snatching a pole-axe from the wall, struck out at Flosi the Burner. This would have ended the case there and then, but one of his guards intercepted the blow and was about to turn the pole-axe on Asgrim, when suddenly Flosi's good temper returned and he shook his head. 'No,' he said, 'leave the old man alone, my friend. After all, it was my fault. I did insult him sorely by coming here, and in any case his action shows courage, for he is one and old while we are many and young.'

So the Burners rode away, leaving old Asgrim still shaking with rage. By his action, it can be seen that Flosi, like other men, had his good points as well as his bad— though few who had loved old Njal would have agreed with this opinion.

19. The Great Trial

Now great chiefs and their followers gathered from all the four quarters of Iceland, and never within living memory had there been so crowded an Althing. Indeed, so determined did some of these men seem, seeking justice, that as they sat on their horses in armed bands in the Upper Field above the Law Rock, Flosi feared for a moment that his case might never reach the court, but would be settled forthwith by sword and axe there on the hillside.

He drew his men together and waited tensely, ready to fight to the last; but the moment passed and the chiefs took their places peacefully, passing to their separate booths to rest before the great trial.

Now Flosi did something which was to bring disaster on him, if he had only known. Realising that he and his followers were soon to pit their wits against the best judges in the land, he went seeking a lawyer who would be both unscrupulous and clever enough to defend them. He found such a one in Eyjolf Bolverksson.

This Eyjolf was a handsome, tall, strong man, who commanded respect from all who came before him. Moreover, he was considered to be one of the three best lawyers in Iceland at that time. However, he suffered from one fault—he loved money above all things and such a passion can sometimes lead to disaster.

At first Eyjolf pretended not to be interested in taking on Flosi's case and replied very coolly to his request.

THE BURNING OF NJAL

When Flosi persisted, Eyjolf even flared up and said that he would not be used as a cat's-paw merely to serve another man's purpose.

Flosi felt that this haggling had gone far enough and he nodded quietly to two of his biggest henchmen. They were named Hallbjorn and Bjarni, and together they could have pulled a tree down, or brought a stallion to his knees. Gently, they stepped over to Eyjolf, lifted him up like a child, and then sat him down on a bench between them, leaning on him not quite hard enough to break his bones. Then Hallbjorn smiled at him and said, 'Just sit with us for a while and see how you feel, friend.'

Eyjolf already knew how he felt. He was wearing a gold band round his head, a scarlet cloak over his shoulders, and holding a silver-studded axe in his hands—but somehow these things gave him no confidence at all now. The sweat was like pearls on his forehead.

Indeed, he was greatly relieved when Flosi spoke to him again and said, 'Great Chief, it is always a pleasure to make friends with such as you. See, I would like to offer you this bracelet as a token of our new friendship. Now, what do you think of it?'

The bracelet was of heavy gold and so well-made that its value must have been at least 1,200 yards of the best homespun cloth and, when Eyjolf looked at it, his grasping hands wanted to reach out and seize it without further delay.

Big Hallbjorn took the bracelet and rammed it himself on to Eyjolf's arm. 'Aye,' he said in his thick voice, 'it quite suits you, Chief.'

Eyjolf had the gold on his arm and moreover he had two fierce men holding him in; he was persuaded.

'Well,' he said, putting on a wise face, 'after the great courtesy you have all shown me, I consider it only right to accept your gift, Flosi. And for my part you can rest assured I will do all in my power to plead your defence. However, I would be pleased if you did not mention to anyone that you had given me this bracelet. You know how some folk get the wrong idea? They might even say I had accepted a bribe from you.'

Flosi nodded wisely and said, 'I understand, friend. Some men will say anything that comes into their heads, won't they, Hallbjorn?'

Big Hallbjorn nodded, 'Aye, master,' he answered, 'and they don't care who gets hurt by their blustering ways, do they, Bjarni?'

As for Eyjolf, he was glad when the three had left his booth and he could feel if all his bones were still whole.

When he had got his breath back again, he strolled over to the booth of Snorri the Priest, a stern chieftain and a great judge, to pass the time of day. Snorri was a sharp-eyed man, as such an Iceland chief needed to be, and the first thing he said was, 'I see you have a new bracelet. Did you buy it or is it a gift from someone?'

Eyjolf was in no mood to discuss this bracelet any further and turned away in embarrassment. Snorri called after him, 'That answers my question. Well, you know what sort of gift it is; I only hope it does not cost you your life, as well as your good name as a lawyer.'

It was not long before the news of that gold bracelet spread among Kari's supporters, for Snorri worried it over with Gizur the White, two dogs with a meaty bone, and Gizur was on the side of Njal's family.

What chiefly worried Kari was that Flosi's new lawyer

had a great reputation, and he had no wish to see the Burners wriggle out of the trap now for the price of a bracelet, however handsome.

So Kari and his party went quietly round the booths, seeking support from the chieftains who would vote at the Althing. Some men still remembered the insulting words of dead Skarp-Hedin and so felt no desire to avenge him, though in fact they bore no love for Flosi. The best offer of help they got was from crafty Snorri the Priest, who frowned a great deal and warned them that the case was likely to end in fighting; but he promised that, provided Kari and his supporters did not start the conflict, he, Snorri, would do his best for them.

'Let the other side begin the combat if they so desire,' he said, staring into the palm of his right hand as though he was reading a book of runes. 'And then see that you retreat to my booth here, where I will have my own doughtiest fighters drawn up and waiting to defend you.'

'Yes,' said Kari, 'but suppose Flosi starts the fight, and then draws off to his stronghold in the mountain? Are we to follow them and battle it out?'

Snorri shut the palm of his hand quickly. It caught a fly. Snorri was always as lucky as that; what other men had to strive for, he obtained by a thoughtless movement of the fingers.

He smiled like an old fox and said, 'If Flosi ever got to the mountain, no man could dislodge him—not even you, Kari, nor your wise friend, Asgrim here. So, I will post other warriors to guard the pass and then he will not escape you.'

Kari and Asgrim said how generous the chief was, but

Snorri waved their thanks aside and went on, 'But, do not forget, I have a reputation for impartiality to keep up, my friends. I do not want to become involved too much in your affair, you understand. My men will only be there to see that you get your fair dues, and not to take action on my own behalf. Therefore, if it does come to fighting, see that you kill no more of the Burners than you can afford to pay blood-money for, since it will be your bargain not mine. And when you have reached the limit of your purse, give me a sign and I will suddenly appear and call an end to the fighting.'

Kari and his supporters left that booth lighter in heart. Once you have one great man to support you, others will soon follow; and after that Kari was not short of promises to help.

So at length the court opened and Flosi stood accused of burning Bergthorsknoll and all in it.

That afternoon there was much applause for Kari and his suit, and when the court disbanded for the night Flosi went gloomily to his lawyer, Eyjolf, and said, 'Well, have I any defence against this?'

Eyjolf shook his head. 'None, I am afraid. After all, you *did* burn the farmstead and all in it. That is an established fact, as we must agree.'

Flosi's eyes grew round with anger. 'What about that gold bracelet I gave you?' he began.

Eyjolf silenced him with a wave of his hand. 'Do not get so anxious, friend,' he said calmly. 'We cannot beat them on fact but we can on legal procedure.'

Flosi scratched his head and said, 'This is beyond me, I am a warrior not a lawyer.'

Eyjolf nodded and smiled. 'Of course,' he said. 'Let

me explain simply; if a boy steals a basket of fish and
confesses to his father, what happens?'

Flosi said, 'Why, his father will beat him, surely?'

Eyjolf nodded. 'That is correct,' he said. 'Now, if that
boy goes to *another boy's father* and tells *him* instead, what
will happen?'

'Why, nothing,' answered Flosi, 'because this other
father has no right to punish him, whatever he has done.'

Eyjolf gave a great sigh of satisfaction and even patted
Flosi on the shoulder. 'Good, good!' he said. 'You are
half a lawyer already!'

Flosi said, 'Perhaps I am not so clever as you think for I
do not see where this is getting us.'

Eyjolf sat down and drew up a stool for Flosi to join
him. Then, leaning forward so that no passer-by should
hear, he said, 'At the moment, we stand before the Eastfirthers' Court, because that is the court which tries all
cases in the district over which you are the chieftain. Is
that not so?'

Flosi nodded. 'Yes, of course that is so.'

'Well,' said Eyjolf, 'suppose you gave up your chieftainship to your brother Thorgeir, and you yourself joined
the following of, say, Chief Askel of Reykjardale, in the
north quarter, would you not then be outside the judgement
of the Eastfirthers' Court?'

Light began to dawn, and Flosi said, 'Why, yes! Then I
could not be tried by the present judges and jury! Their
case would fall to the ground for having brought it before
the wrong court! Now I see what you meant about the
boy who stole the fish. Why, Eyjolf, I feel that I shall be
getting good value for the bracelet, after all.'

Eyjolf said, 'You have not reached the bottom of the

barrel yet, friend. Don't you see, if Mord and Kari and
their friends plead their case in the wrong court, they
not only forfeit that case, but they commit contempt of
court and so will have to stand trial themselves, at our
new Fifth Court, which is meant for all cases that cannot
be brought before the Quarter Courts!'

Flosi almost ran to offer his chieftaincy to his brother
and then to join the band of Askel of Reykjardale. And when
this was done, in secret, he began to look forward to the
next day's trial with great glee.

Now this was to be the crucial day but unfortunately in
the night Kari's lawyer Thorhall found that his boil
had swelled so much that by dawn he was in such agony
that he did not dare shift from his bed. All the same, he
told Kari that if he needed legal help that day, he would
send the correct advice by a swift messenger.

When the court opened there was a festive war-mood
about it, for all the men on both sides had turned up in
their coloured clothes and fighting-gear, with war-tokens
in their helmets.

Mord of Hof began his charge against Flosi and three
times Eyjolf stopped the proceedings on the grounds that
the jury was either biased or unqualified to sit in judgement.
And three times word was sent to groaning Thorhall, who
returned such advice that crafty Eyjolf was defeated—
which greatly pleased the listening crowds and called
forth their cheers.

In fact many men began to whisper that Flosi had no
case at all and was only trying to gain time by quibbling.
It was not long before the foreman of the jury announced
a verdict of guilty against Flosi, whose turn it was now to
state his defence.

Lawyer Eyjolf wasted no words. He said confidently, 'Our defence is simply as follows: this jury has no jurisdiction over Flosi, who is at this moment a Thingman of Askel and is therefore bound only by the judgement of the North Quarter Court. This case is closed.'

As he sat down, smiling, silence fell over the meadow and then a great muttering rose that Flosi had outwitted them all in the end.

Once more word was sent to Thorhall, who was biting the coverlets with pain now. Yet he rose in his bed and said, 'Very well, we must counter trickery with trickery. Now we must drop our original case and instead summon both Flosi and Eyjolf for giving and taking bribes in court. The penalty for that is only three years' outlawry; but we can get a verdict of lifetime outlawry if we can prove that these two have committed contempt of the new Fifth Court by having used any evidence which had nothing to do with the original case at issue. I mean, by Flosi's gift of his chieftaincy to his brother, for example.'

Mord of Hof now stood before the court and said, 'I charge Flosi Thordarson with bribing Eyjolf Bolverksson to defend him in court here, and I demand a sentence of three years' outlawry on him, unless he pays his guilt-fine for the burning of Njal's farm and family immediately. On this count alone, I claim that all his possessions be forfeit. Now, should Flosi not meet this claim, I further demand that he be sentenced to outlawry for life. And this charge and claim I shall refer to the Fifth Court, where it now belongs since my earlier pleas have been slighted here in the Quarter Court, causing me to seek a higher authority.'

Then he and Asgrim wasted no more time, but quickly

left the Law Rock and went to the Fifth Court, leaving
Flosi, Eyjolf and the judges still casually arguing in the
Quarter Court, carried away by their discussion.

Eyjolf was the first to realise that by their delay they had
allowed the two accusers an advantage. 'What fools we
were, to be so occupied,' he said, 'while Mord and Asgrim
were getting in their new plea! Well, there may still be
a chance of outwitting them, friend Flosi, although they
think they can prove a case against us. Thorhall may be a
fine lawyer, but not even he can foresee all points that may
crop up.'

Though they hurried, they were barely in time to prepare
a defence, for Mord was in full stride and, having put
his case, demanded an immediate verdict of guilty in the
Fifth Court.

At this point, one of the judges spoke to the over-hasty
Mord and said, 'Your enthusiasm does you credit, Mord,
and I do not notice that the accused has any defence to
put forward against the plea. But we must be correct in
all things, and I have to inform you that, according to
our law in this court, there are too many judges present. I
have counted forty-eight of them, whereas, for a case of
this sort, only thirty-six are allowed to bring in a verdict.'

Eyjolf rubbed his hands and laughed quietly. 'Ah,
Flosi,' he whispered, 'this is the rock on which his ship
may founder at last!'

Flosi shook his head. 'Oh, you lawyers!' he said. 'I am
lost in it all like a fly in a spider's web. What does it mean?'

Eyjolf said, 'It means this: Mord must now request
six judges to withdraw, naming them separately, and then
must invite us to do the same, so bringing the number
down to its legal proportions.'

Flosi said, 'It may be plain to you, my friend, but to me it is as clear as mud!'

The lawyer smiled and answered, 'Ah, well, a man cannot have everything in this world. After all, you are a brave fighter.' Then, observing a certain look in Flosi's eye, he went on quickly, 'You see, Mord will exclude his six judges and will ask us to do the same. But we will only go round the field, looking at one or another and mumbling, and, in his anxiety to be on with the trial, he may never notice that we do not call on our six to leave the court.'

And it turned out just as Eyjolf said. Mord cut down the number of judges but, in his haste, paid little heed to what his opponents were doing. And when, triumphantly, Mord demanded a verdict of guilty, Eyjolf stepped forward and said, 'May it please the court, my opponent has, unfortunately, just made a serious mistake. In spite of the chieftain's warnings, he has pressed forward with his case before forty-two judges, instead of a court of thirty-six. Now, justice is justice, as we all know; but the law is the law, and may not be set aside by the mistake of an over-hasty pleader. If our law, of which we are all proud, is to be preserved, then this Althing may not permit it to be put aside by one man, however honest he may think himself to be. In other words, if our court, properly formed, is held to be of thirty-six judges, then a court of forty-two judges *is not that court*—and so may not give judgement on Flosi.'

At this, the crowds began to chatter and even the judges looked confused, for in the haste and the crush of the whole proceedings few of them had noticed everything that had gone on.

Then Eyjolf held up his hand for silence, and his gold bracelet glimmered mockingly in the sunlight. 'Furthermore,' he said, 'not only is Mord's case completely destroyed, but, by pleading so hastily before an improperly-formed court, despite warning from the chieftains and lawgivers, Mord Valgardsson of Hof has placed himself and those he speaks for in the greatest peril. In fact, he has openly shown his contempt of our law and of this court, the penalty for which is that his earlier manslaughter action must be dismissed, and all his companions in this case be sentenced to outlawry for life.'

At this, Mord began to shake, for he realised now how terribly he had blundered.

As for Snorri the Priest, who had promised help to Kari and his friends, he sent a message out to his warriors instructing them to ride swiftly to the mountain pass, to cut off any retreat that Flosi and the Burners would soon make. 'For,' he whispered, 'the way things are going now, it will not be long before words are discarded and swords jump from the scabbard!'

While Snorri sent to his fighting-men, Mord sent anxiously to Thorhall on his bed of pain, telling him of the turn of events and begging his instant instructions.

But Thorhall was speechless to think how he had been outwitted and to think that now, by the simplest of legal errors, his foster-father Njal would go unavenged.

With a deep groan, he got up and, despite the agony, snatched from the wall of his booth a spear which Skarp-Hedin had given him, an heirloom.

'The time has come for getting out of bed,' he said. 'A man cannot lie thinking for ever. Things need to be done.'

As he spoke, he drove the spear deep into his swollen

leg to lance the boil. The green floor of his booth was suddenly flooded with crimson. Skarp-Hedin's spear knew where to search. It needed no hand to guide it.

'Agh!' said Thorhall, clenching his teeth as he withdrew the sharp iron.

Then, striding through the door without even a limp and so fast that the messenger could not keep up with him, Thorhall headed straight for the Fifth Court.

Only one man stood in his path, Grim the Red, one of Flosi's fiercest kinsmen. 'Oh, oh!' said Grim, 'and where are you off to, Lawyer?'

Thorhall said, 'I thought I would go for a walk since it is a fine day.'

Then lunging forward with the spear, he split Grim's waiting shield, so that the keen point stood out a hand's length behind the man's shoulder-blades. Thorhall glanced coldly at him, and with a twist of the wrists, flung him off the spike as a brisk fisherman does his catch.

Kari, waiting at the court, saw this and turned open-mouthed to Thorhall's father, Asgrim. 'By the Lord,' he said, 'but your son wastes no time!'

Asgrim smiled bleakly. 'He always comes quickly to the point,' he answered. 'It is his legal training. Come, let us start the battle, friend. We have delayed long enough already.'

20. The Fight at the Althing

JUST as when an autumn wind blows upon a heap of leaves, red and brown and yellow, driving them here and there, sweeping them into ragged heaps, swirling them about one another in coloured frenzy, so Kari and his friends, Thorgeir, Asgrim, his son Thorhall, Gizur the White and Mord, blew hard upon Flosi and the Burners. The hills and meadows where the law had been announced for generations now echoed to fierce shouts and the stern clash of weapons.

Men fought everywhere, in small parties up and down the slopes, each in a small and bloody world of his own. Anger was high on both sides, blinding the fighters to what they were doing. Now the sober words of judge and jury were cast away, and the only verdicts were given by spear, sword and axe.

Kari did hard work that day: turning, twisting and jumping in the air to avoid blows, he put the spear into many and left them stark. From him, the fierce warriors Hallbjorn and Bjarni limped away, knowing only too well they had at last met their master. Thorgeir, flailing about with Skarp-Hedin's famous axe, laid men low as a reaper does with his scythe at harvest time. Asgrim, Thorhall and Gizur sought Flosi and his closest companions, and after a fierce exchange of blows, sent them running over the Axewater River and towards their stronghold of Almanna Gorge.

And they might even have escaped but that, true to his promise, Snorri the Priest and all his men suddenly appeared, barring their flight.

'Well, then,' he called out to Flosi, 'you seem to be in a great hurry. Who can be chasing you, to put such speed into your legs?'

Breathing hard, Flosi replied, 'As though you don't know! And now you are stopping us from getting away to safety.'

Snorri the Priest smiled mockingly and said, 'Don't blame me, my friend. Instead, blame those two old scoundrels, Thorvald Cropped-Beard and Slave Kol.'

Flosi gazed in astonishment. 'But why bring up those two?' he asked. 'They have been dead for generations.'

Snorri put on a wise look, and nodding, answered, 'Aye, I know: but their evil spirits still seem to hang about this place, upsetting people.'

Then he turned to his warriors and said, 'Very well, the time has come, as I told you. Get about your work and drive Flosi and the Burners back down the hill to their pursuers. It is their duty to settle this affair, once and for all. Let justice thrive!'

Soon, howling like hounds after a stag, Kari's men were on them again, harrying them hither and thither, and cutting them down whenever they met.

Kari was able to do one satisfactory thing that day: seeing Eyjolf running, trying to save his life and his gold bracelet, he snatched a spear from a man who stood near by and, taking aim, put all thoughts of gold out of the lawyer's mind for ever.

And so ended the fight at the Althing, for now the

Burners had no more stomach for it, or for arguing any further on points of legal procedure.

Snorri and other great chiefs came up and suggested that it would be wiser for them to return to the court and accept a final judgement there, rather than taking sword-verdict or spear-sentence.

And this they did, after dressing their wounds, and carrying their dead to church. Flosi and the Burners were in no mood to argue about anything and it was not long before the court reached its final verdict. This was as follows: Njal was awarded a triple-fine; Bergthora, Grim and Helgi a double-fine; and all other men who were murdered by burning, a single-fine, with the exception of Skarp-Hedin. His death was not paid for by Flosi, but was set off against the death of Hoskuld, who was killed when he was out sowing corn that morning in his scarlet cloak.

So much for the money-compensation; but there was more to follow. Flosi and most of the remaining Burners were ordered to leave Iceland and serve a sentence of three years as outlaws: but four of the most bloodthirsty of the band were outlawed for life, and were forbidden ever again to return to their native land. These men were Gunnar Lambason, Grani Gunnarsson, Glum Hildisson and Kol Thorsteinsson.

Then the court broke up and most of the judges felt that a very satisfactory settlement had been reached to a most difficult problem.

But as they rode home together, Kari and Thorgeir still frowned. Thorgeir said, 'No amount of money can bring Njal and Skarp-Hedin back, friend.'

Kari's brows were as black as an Iceland winter cloud.

'I was thinking that,' he said. 'It is very well for the judges to go happily to their meat and drink and warm fires as though they have settled everything and have earned a quiet life. But Flosi and his henchmen are still alive and laughing. To men like that, three years of outlawry will be like a holiday not a punishment.'

They rode on a while in silence. Then Thorgeir said, 'I still have Skarp-Hedin's axe.'

Kari nodded. 'I know,' he said quietly. 'Don't interrupt me; I am thinking.'

Thorgeir said, 'And so am I. It would not take the wisest man in the world to say what it is we are both thinking.'

Kari allowed himself to smile, but it was not a pleasant smile. He said, 'No, it wouldn't, would it?'

21. The Hunting Begins

THOUGHTS of vengeance bite as deeply into the heart as a sword. Like hounds on the scent, Kari and Thorgeir followed the track of the Burners and soon heard from some wandering women by the roadside that the Sigfusson clan, numbering fifteen riders, were not far away.

Thorgeir said to Kari, 'How many of them should we kill, would you say?'

Kari answered wryly, 'I will name no number, for those murdered with the mouth often live the longest. We must just do our best, friend.'

Along the Kerlingardale River, which rolled down in full spate, the two found the Sigfussons sleeping in a hollow with their spears stuck in the ground near by. Kari and Thorgeir quietly dismounted, then drew out the spears gently and flung them into the river with scarcely a splash.

Said Thorgeir, 'Shall we wake them first?'

Kari smiled and nodded. 'I am sure that neither of us wants to kill them in their sleep,' he said. 'That would be dishonourable.'

So they both gave a great shout, then, as the men jumped up in alarm, stood back and gave them time to find helmets and axes. And when the fifteen seemed ready, the two avengers drove in at them. Now no quarter was given and in this surprise attack Kari and Thorgeir put an end to five of the enemy. Skarp-Hedin's old axe, 'Battle-Troll', did harsh work that day, biting both with blade and horn and, in one stroke, ending two men at once. Then, staggered by such fighting furies, the Sigfussons ran blindly to their horses and galloped away.

'Hey, wait a while,' shouted Thorgeir, 'we haven't finished with you yet!'

But the Sigfussons had forgotten their manners and did not answer this invitation.

When they arrived at Flosi's farmstead at Svinafell and told their story, the chieftain laughed, almost as though he was merry, and said, 'Well, and what did you expect from those two? Let this be a warning to you, never to sleep in hollows in future. The grass is damp there and a man might catch a chill that would carry him off!'

The two avengers now rode back to Holt, and Thorgeir sent his brothers away from home so that they should not become involved in whatever might happen next. But in the steading he kept thirty fighting-men about him in case the Burners should now pay a return visit to those who had so humbled them.

Flosi by this time was too wily for that though, and tried to reach some sort of settlement with the two. At the back of his mind he thought that if he could somehow separate Kari and Thorgeir it would then make life easier until he could sail away.

Grani Gunnarsson and Gunnar Lambason said, 'Once we get Kari on his own, our fear will dwindle and we can deal with him!'

A man standing by said bitterly, 'If you believe that, you will believe anything. If five men went into a pit with a bear, do you think they would come out again unhurt?'

All the same, in the end Thorgeir, who now felt that

he had avenged Njal, agreed to come to peace with the Burners, provided Kari was allowed to stay on undisturbed at Holt.

Kari's comment was: 'You suit yourself, Thorgeir. As for me, I still remember that a little son of mine was burned that night at Bergthorsknoll, and no amount of money will bring him back. I shall make no peace with them, ever.'

When Flosi heard of this, he said, 'I cannot blame him. I would say the same in his place—that is, if I had Kari's courage.'

This much must be said of Flosi, that he had many good qualities. After all, when he burned Njal, he did so to avenge Hoskuld; and, let men remember, he did give Njal, the women and the children a chance to leave before the burning began.

All the same, Kari was not the man to weigh such things in the balance. His mind was set, and soon he went to Thorgeir and said, 'This peace bores me, friend. I must be out and doing and I cannot stay under your roof if I am to prune the branches that still stick out! Otherwise, men would say you were in the affair, too. So, forgive me, but I must be on my way.'

When he left, he took his weapons, as would be expected, a change of clothes, plenty of ready money in gold and silver, and two horses. These would suffice, he thought, for the hunting that was still to do. Thorgeir wept to see him go but knew him too well to try to keep him from the course he had set.

22. Full Cry!

Now at Mork there lived a little man named Bjorn, who was good-hearted and quite well-off but rather boastful about his strength and skill with weapons. In fact, he was not the bravest or the briskest fighter in Iceland—but he felt that he had to praise himself because his wife Valgerd was always so scornful of him, comparing him with other men who carried war wounds and had been in many fights. 'Oh, you can run fast enough,' taunted Valgerd, 'but who wants a runner for a husband? You might as well be a flute player!'

The worst wound Bjorn carried was a white mark down the neck where the cat had scratched him; but there is this to say, he drove that cat over the farmyard fence and no mistake, when his temper was roused and he had found a long broom-stick.

It was to Bjorn's house that wandering Kari now came, seeking shelter while he made his plans. Valgerd was glad enough to welcome the warrior and have a man in the house, as she put it, at last.

Kari stayed with them for a week and Bjorn was most helpful to him, spying for him and bringing back the news that Flosi and his Burners were at last making ready to ride to the coast and take ships for their outlawry abroad.

One night by the fireside Kari said to Bjorn, more in jest than anything else, 'I, too, am thinking of breathing a little sea air. I would like to see what it is like abroad myself.'

'How would you go?' asked Valgerd.

Kari shrugged and said, 'Well, I think the best way would be through Flosi's country, over the mountains, then down to Alptafjord.'

Valgerd said, 'You have picked a dangerous route, surely?'

And as she spoke, she half-turned her head and gave Bjorn a contemptuous look.

Bjorn said stoutly, 'Aye, it is a dangerous route but not too dangerous for sharp fellows like myself and Kari, eh, Kari?'

The stern warrior's eyes opened wide with surprise but he smiled and nodded. 'I think we could manage it, if we were careful,' he said. Then he went to bed.

When he had gone, Valgerd said to her husband, 'My man, if you let this fine fellow down now, it will be the last you see of me. I promise you that.'

Bjorn said airily, 'Pooh! Pooh! You are soon going to learn what it is like to be married to a real fighting-man, my good woman.'

Valgerd said, 'We shall see. Yes, we shall see.'

The next morning, the two men rode away and after a while stopped in the hills in enemy country. Kari was in a teasing mood now and said to Bjorn, 'Well, warrior, suppose our foes swoop down on us now—what are we to do?'

Bjorn's eyes almost jumped out of their lids. 'Why,' he stammered, 'we should leap on to our horses and ride off!' Then he thought again and said, 'I beg your pardon, I was speaking without due consideration. No, we should hide behind these rocks and then rush out and kill any stragglers before they saw us. That is the best plan, don't you think, Kari?'

Kari nodded. 'I shall leave it to you, with all your experience in these matters,' he said. 'You can take over for a while.'

That night, Bjorn didn't get a wink of sleep for worrying.

The next day they rode down to Skaptrivertongue and there before them lay some of the enemy resting. When Bjorn began to shudder, Kari took him by the arm and said, 'Yes, it is a bit chilly this morning, but we shall soon get warmed up. Look, friend, we will quietly take up our position on that little headland that sticks out into the river and I want you to stand behind me and not expose yourself too much. Just make yourself as useful as you can.'

Bjorn drew a deep breath and said, 'Mercy on us! I never thought to use another man as my shield, Kari. But since you insist I must agree to your wishes. No doubt I shall find the opportunity to put my brains and dash to some use.'

'No doubt,' said Kari, grinning. 'Come on, let us begin.'

It was not long before the fighting started, and then Kari put paid to Lambi Sigurdarson, Thorstein Geirleifsson and Gunnar of Skal, besides wounding Grani Gunnarsson so deeply in the thigh that his comrades had to drag him from the battle to save his life.

Bjorn did what he could, too; when one of the enemy ran up from behind to chop at Kari's legs, Bjorn struck the man such a blow that it was easy for Kari to spare a moment and finish him.

Not one of the Burners in that band escaped without a

wound of some sort and, when they had jumped on to
their horses and safely fled, Bjorn jeered after them as such
cowards deserved.

'That's the way!' said Kari, joining in and hooting at
the distant riders. 'That will teach them!'

'Mm,' said Bjorn, thoughtfully, 'I hadn't the heart to
finish off Grani Gunnarsson when you pricked him in the
leg. Although, frankly, I think he would have deserved it.'

Kari said, 'Well, it won't be long now before they are
back, then you will have another chance to show your
skill. What, friend Bjorn, do you think we ought to do
when they come?'

Bjorn clenched his hands to stop them shaking and said,
'Well, in my opinion, we ought to pretend to ride north,
then swing about under cover of the hill and ride south.
That should fool them!'

'I agree,' said Kari. 'Why, you took the very words
out of my mouth!'

'Oh, never fear,' answered Bjorn, 'I have as much brains
as bravery. You can depend on that; aye, that you can.'

Kari nodded, a little weary now of the man's boasting.
He said, 'Right, brave one, keep watch while I go to
sleep for a while. If I am wanted, wake me, but not unless
it is strictly necessary.'

He had hardly closed his eyes, when Bjorn was shaking
him by the shoulder and saying, 'For pity's sake, wake up!
They are on us!'

Kari yawned and opened his eyes slowly. 'Where?' he
asked.

Bjorn pointed towards some small specks on the hillside. 'There!' he said. 'Now what shall we do?'

Kari led him to an overhanging crag of rock and said,

'Get under there and stand behind me with a shield. Or, if that does not suit you, mount your horse and be away as fast as you can spur.'

Bjorn thought it over, then said, 'What! Leave you in the lurch! Everyone would say I was a coward then—besides, if I *did* ride away, one of them would soon catch me. I'll stay, Kari.'

For a moment, it looked as though the foe were going to ride past the overhanging crag and Bjorn breathed a deep sigh; but suddenly six men turned as though they had heard him and came right at Kari.

This time, Bjorn had quick luck; Glum Hildisson lunged at Kari with a spear, missed him and struck the rock instead. Immediately, Bjorn swiped out and hacked the point off the spear—after which, Kari finished that piece of work. Two more drove in, and received scythe-like death-blows from the warrior, by which time both Kari and Bjorn had taken a wound or two themselves.

The rest of the attackers rode away then, and told Flosi of their losses. He shook his head and said, 'I swear, where in Iceland is there a man to compare with Kari now?'

He spoke no ill of the hunter; indeed, though Kari was coming towards him all the time, wading through blood, Flosi was getting to love this warrior for his stark courage, just as a hawk might admire and respect the hovering eagle that means to kill him.

Among warriors, this is no strange thing; they are not like other men, and, by some logic of the gods, they often love each other best when they are face to face in combat.

That night Kari conducted Bjorn back to Mork, having made the impression on his enemies that he wished, and there he delivered the honest fellow to his wife. At the stack-yard gate, Bjorn said, 'Please come in, Kari, and tell my wife what we have done, in your own words. She would never believe me.'

Kari slapped him on the shoulder. 'Certainly, old warrior,' he said. 'Lead the way.'

So Bjorn swaggered into the kitchen and said to his wife as she bent over the fire, 'Well, woman, we are back, and I must tell you that there has been a bit of trouble.'

Valgerd looked beyond her husband, smiling, and said to Kari, 'Did you find him useful at all? I don't suppose you did!'

Kari's face was as stiff and cold as stone. He answered the woman and said, 'A man's back is bare without a brother. Your husband has dealt with three men himself. He carries a wound. See that you look after him, and show that you deserve to have such a hero in your house.'

Valgerd stared at Bjorn as though she had never seen him before. And from that moment, he was master in his own house, and both he and his wife were all the better for that.

Little did proud and happy Bjorn know that Kari later took the trouble to ride over to Holt, where Thorgeir was master, and tell his old friend all that had happened.

'What do you want me to do?' asked Thorgeir, smiling.

'I want you to watch over that little fellow and see that no one comes and hurts him, now that he has got what he wants out of life—the respect of his mocking wife.'

Thorgeir said quietly, 'Yes, Kari, I'll do that. But, tell me, what do *you* want out of life?'

Kari's nostrils flared like a stallion's. 'I want nothing less than the deaths of Gunnar Lambason the Burner, and Kol Thorsteinsson the Burner. That much would pacify me, brother, for it would bring my score up to fifteen men, which I calculate to be the equivalent of those who were roasted in the farm fire, together with my little son, Thord, who had done no harm to anyone in his short life, and whose spirit would weep at his father's door until the end of time unless I went on along the road my feet have already taken.'

Thorgeir said, 'I shall not try to dissuade you, brother. You know what must be done. Flosi and the rest of the Burners are soon to sail abroad, to begin their period of outlawry. You will not catch them here in Iceland.'

When Kari smiled it was as though a white skull, dug from the ground, had opened its bony jaws. 'I know that, brother,' he said. 'Where they go, there shall I go, but always a pace behind, and always with the blade in my hand. I shall be to them like a shadow, but not a black one, a red one. And at the end they will wish that they had never put the flame to Njal's steading. Either that, or that they had lain down with him, that red night, beneath the damp ox-hide, and perished gently. They shall come to think that, of the two, Njal had the better bargain in the end. I, Kari, tell you this, and it is as true as the sky, the rocks, the black-backed gulls and Rang River.'

Thorgeir said, 'You do not need to tell me this, brother. I am a fighting-man, too. I know how it is. Good fortune go with you.'

23. View Halloo!

IT was a stormy season when Flosi and the remaining
Burners rode east to Hornafjord and there bought a longship, in return for a portion of land, from a Trondheim
sailor named Eyjolf Nose, who wished to marry and to
settle down in Iceland. It was a good ship and could hold
not only all Flosi's followers, but also their goods and
supplies, enough to see most of them through their three
years of wandering in outlawry. They set forth as soon
as the wind changed, though many on board feared that
the seas would be hard to face, and they were not wrong.

Kari followed them in a ship belonging to Kolbein the
Black, an Orkney man who often made the run up to
Iceland and knew every shoal and skerry on the way.
Some men said that he knew all the black-backed gulls
and the sad-eyed seals, too; but some men will say anything. What is true is that Kolbein the Black was a great
fighting viking who always stood by his passengers. He
swore to help Kari in his search, and putting his great
arms round him, even promised to die for him if the need
arose.

Kari pulled the man's red ears and said, 'That is a
pretty speech, out of an honest mouth, Shipmaster, and
I shall not forget it. But I hope that the only dying to be
done will be on their ship, and not ours! Come on, let us
fare forth: we shall not kill men by walking up and down
the beach!'

They pushed off from Eyrar, exactly a fortnight after Flosi had set sail. The clouds were black, the wind was screaming in the rigging, the deep-green waves hissed at the ship and slapped her rolling planks with the blows of a giant's hand. Two black birds followed Kari's ship until she was out of land-sight.

Kolbein pointed to them and said, 'They know how many men will be killed. Two birds for two men.'

Kari's lips were drawn tightly together and his grizzled beard jutted out. He answered, 'See to the steering, Master Kolbein, and I will see to the killing.'

Across his knees he held a new sword, given to him as a parting gift by Gizur the White. It had a fine pommel of jet, and silver wires bound round the wooden handle. Its long, broad blade glinted blue in the autumn sunlight and its centre runnel was inlaid with the curling shapes of serpents. It was such a sword as would last for ten generations and, with careful use, might never need to be re-ground. Kari was so proud of it he did not even dare name it yet, lest he should choose a title unworthy of it.

Kolbein smiled at him and said, 'Perhaps you will christen your baby at Yuletide, Kari. Even now, down in the South Isles, they will be fattening the pigs and scrubbing the table-tops to be ready for the feasting.'

Kari made his new sword whistle through the bleak salt air. 'There will be some who sit down at the clean table who do not finish their meal,' he said.

Kolbein staggered back to the steerboard over the lurching deck. 'And there may be some who never get within sight of the table,' he said to himself, seeing the spume-ridged black mountains of water that lay before them, range upon range.

It was hard-going that autumn but, a little while before Yuletide, Flosi's storm-battered longship put in at Hrossey in the Orkneys, glad to have passed unscathed though gales and fogs.

Here Earl Sigurd was the lord, a grim man who knew of the Burning and thought little of the Burners. But, in the end, he gave Flosi a place in his crowded hall, and let the band of Icelanders sit at his Yuletide feasting.

It was Yule-day itself when Kari and Kolbein landed on Orkney and, seeing the bright lights burning in the great feast-hall, crept quietly towards the open windows to hear what was going on there.

Gunnar Lambason, with an ale-cup in his hand, was sitting before the dais on which Earl Sigurd sat between his chief guests, and was telling the tale of Njal's burning in rough verse, making it seem like an heroic adventure. One of the guests asked, 'What of that big man, Skarp-Hedin? Now, how did he take it?'

Gunnar laughed in scorn and answered, 'Oh, well enough when we started—but he was weeping before it was all over!' The hall was full of rough laughter.

A man can stand only so much and now Kari's patience left him. Suddenly he ran into the hall, his new sword in his hand, and shouted out, 'You have heard these brave warriors boasting how they burned an old man, an old woman and a little child—but have you heard how they have spent their time since? I will tell you that part of the story: their days have been passed, running up and down Iceland with a man after them, and always followed by ravens who knew that once this man caught them there would be meat to eat.'

The Burners gazed at Kari as though he was a ghost.

Earl Sigurd said harshly, 'And you, who burst into my hall with a drawn sword—who are you?'

Kari yelled, 'I am the man who follows them!'

Then, with great bounds, he ran the length of the hall, and before Gunnar Lambason could rise from his chair, swept out with his new sword. Gunnar's head left his shoulders and rolled down the table in front of the Earl and his noble guests.

'Hold that man!' ordered the Earl. 'He shall die for disturbing our Yuletide feasting in this season of goodwill!'

But no man laid hands on Kari, for his name had gone through the North world, and there were few who did not regard him as a great hero now.

Then Flosi the Burner rose from his place and said to the Earl, 'Kari Solmundarson has good cause for doing this, my lord. I speak up for him here and say that he is a true man, doing his duty. Let him go, Earl Sigurd.'

In the heavy silence that followed these words, Kari strode from the feast-hall, like a fierce hound on stiff legs, smiling at ghosts, and no man there came within two yards of him. He passed into the darkness and was gone. His footsteps made no sound at all.

Thralls came from the kitchens and carried out dead Gunnar. Others scrubbed the table-top, so that the feasting should go on.

Earl Sigurd said, 'There are few men as brave as Kari, to walk into a hall and do what he did.'

Flosi nodded sadly. 'If I could count him among my friends,' he said, 'I should think that God had smiled upon me. But he and I are like oil and water, and we can never mix, it seems.'

Then Flosi took up Gunnar's interrupted tale, and told the true story of the Burning, giving all credit and blame where they were due. In his deep heart, he was a fair-minded man, and the more so as time went on: though there was no man alive who could call him a coward.

Down by the seashore, Kolbein the Black said to Kari, 'Do you recall those two black birds that followed us out of Eyrar? Well, you have now fed one of them.'

Kari wiped his new sword lovingly, and answered, 'Were there only two black birds? I thought there were more. I must be getting forgetful.'

Kolbein shook his black head and said, 'I don't think so, friend. No, I really don't think so.'

Then he went aft and told the steersman to head for Scotland. 'We shall be safer there,' he said, 'and can rest up over the winter at Freswick in Caithness. I have a good old comrade there, called Skeggi, who will shelter us until spring comes.'

Kari slipped his sword away in its calf-skin scabbard and smiled. 'Anywhere will suit me,' he said, 'until it is time to go visiting again.'

24. 'Mort!'

As spring came through the gaunt pines of Caithness and the new lambs tested their legs on the green hill-slopes, Kari sat fidgeting by the hearth-stone, his hair and beard uncombed, speaking to no man.

One bright morning, Kolbein the Black came to him hesitantly and said, 'News has come from Orkney in a fishing-smack. Fifteen of Flosi's men have joined Earl Sigurd's army, to fight in Ireland. But Flosi is not with them: he has sailed south, towards the Welsh coast, a weary man, and has vowed to make a pilgrimage to Rome for the forgiveness of his sins.'

Kari stirred the white ashes for a while with the toe of his shoe. Then he said slowly, 'I am a weary man, too. Revenge burns up a man's heart as fire does wood. Perhaps I should make a pilgrimage to Rome as well.'

He smiled strangely as he said this, and Black Kolbein leaned over him and asked gently, 'Have we come to the end of the journey then, master?'

Kari shook his head and whispered, 'No, friend, not yet; not quite yet.'

He began to play with the sword that Gizur had given him, pulling it from the sheath, then pushing it back again; though now, Kolbein noticed, he did not handle it so lovingly as before.

Then Kari looked up and said softly, 'Did you hear whether Kol Thorsteinsson had gone to Ireland?'

Kolbein smiled knowingly then and replied, 'No, he is one of the few Burners who still sail with Flosi. Why do you ask, is he the next on your list?'

Kari pursed his lips and pushed the sword away from him carelessly. He said, as though thinking of other things, 'It was Kol Thorsteinsson who lit the weed-heap which first set Njal's steading afire. He is a big, strong man, with a thick neck.'

Black Kolbein had lived among warriors all his days, but he had never heard a man speak so coldly before. Just for something to say in that chill silence, he asked, 'Is it Kol Thorsteinsson who must feed the second raven, then?'

But Kari stared back at him as though he had never seen him in his life before. 'You talk too much, sailor,' he said. 'There is a time for talking and a time for doing. Now is the time for sailing southwards towards Wales.'

It was no easy journey, down through the Minch and into the teeth of the spring gales: but Kari made it. From one of the islands, men came out in a curragh and told Kari that there had been a great battle at Clontarf near Dublin in Ireland, and that the fifteen Burners who had gone with Earl Sigurd had died on the field there, among the red heather.

Kari gave the news-bearers a handful of silver and said, 'Their hayfields up in Iceland will go uncut this year, then. I hate to see the good green grass rot on the damp ground.'

The Islanders were rough, rug-headed, red-shanked fellows, who stared at this strange viking with wide grey eyes.

Black Kolbein pushed them away quickly and whispered, 'Get out of his sight, friends. Away with you, in your tarry boat. The master is busy with his thoughts, and who knows what he may think next?'

The Islanders went over the side, chattering in their own strange language, and pulled off as fast as they could, away from the black longship.

When they had gone, Kari turned to Kolbein and said, 'Queer fellows, these Islanders. A man would have thought the Devil was breathing down their necks.'

Black Kolbein coughed behind his hand and said, 'Where am I to sail next, master?'

Kari yawned and said, 'To Wales, where else? There is no work for a man in Ireland these days, I hear, not since Clontarf.'

As magnet draws iron, so does quarry the hunter. On the Welsh coast there was a creek where Flosi's ship lay. Into the next creek down Kari rowed and had his shipmen cover up their vessel with bracken and beech-boughs, the fresh new leaves still on them. Then he set off, his sword under his arm, towards a market town that lay just inland.

'Shall we come with you, master?' asked Black Kolbein.

Kari did not even turn. He said to the ground, 'Haven't you sailors any ropes to splice? Haven't you any seams to caulk? See to your trade and I will see to mine.'

All the same, Kolbein and a handful of sailors followed Kari in case he needed them. But he didn't.

Now in the market place that morning, Kol Thorsteinsson was busy at a money-changer's booth, bartering for silver money.

'Look, you crafty Welsh cur,' he was saying to the booth-keeper, 'I have had the good luck to become betrothed to one of your fine Welsh ladies, and I want to offer her a good marriage settlement in true coinage. So see that you give me the right exchange, or I will take the black thieving head off your bent thieving shoulders!'

Just as the trembling booth-keeper was counting the silver money into the Icelander's outstretched hand, Kari stepped from behind a stall and said, 'Hey, Kol! What a fine morning! How lucky we are!'

Then he slashed out with his new sword at the thickest part of Kol Thorsteinsson's neck. Afterwards the booth-keeper told folk that even as the viking's head lay on the ground, its lips still went on counting up to ten before it was silent. But you know what Welshmen are.

As for Kari, he turned away and saw an open-mouthed apple-woman. 'Go to Flosi, the Chief,' he said, 'and tell him plainly what has been done. None of your Welsh tantrums now, woman: just tell him simply, without any talk about ghosts and magic, and say that Kari Solmundarson did it. Tell him to give this fellow a good burial, since he is the last I shall come for. And keep this for your pains: I shall not use it again this harvest.'

He flung the reeking sword into her lap, among the green apples, then walked like a blind man back towards the creek.

Kolbein and his fellows stood gaping in his way, but he never even noticed them, and they never told him what they had witnessed in the market place.

25. End-blow

———⟨⟩———

EVERY fire burns down: every storm blows itself out:
every harvest is reaped, or rots ungathered back into the
earth.

Flosi paid his homage to the Pope in Rome and, when
his three years as an outlaw were over, sailed home to
Iceland and lived quietly at Svinafell.

Kari's ship took another course, leading him at first to
Normandy, among folk who spoke much the same language
as himself, and who told him how to reach Rome and to
get absolution from the Holy Father for all his past sins.
And this he did at last.

It was while he was abroad that news reached him of
his wife's death; she who was called Helga, the daughter
of old Njal.

And so, wearily, like Flosi, he sailed back to Iceland,
the only home he knew.

It was late in the year, a time when shrill voices
shrieked at sailormen from the scudding black clouds,
and when great-shouldered trolls pushed up under the
deck-planks of the stoutest longship, trying to turn it
turtle.

No man in his senses would have made the Iceland-run
in such a season; but Kari was Kari. And though sea-luck
was with him, sitting on his right shoulder, land-luck
taunted him. In a night as black as the inside of a charcoal-
burner's bag, Kari's ship was flung sideways ashore and

stove in, at Ingolfshead, just below Flosi's steading at Svinafell.

Though all the crew were saved, some of them thought their time on dry land would be short, having been delivered so neatly by fate into the mouse-trap.

Worst of all, it was snowing when they landed, in the way that it can only snow in Iceland.

But Kari did not seem to care now.

'What is to be, will be, lads,' he said, leading the way up from the shore. 'Let us walk on to Flosi's steading and see how he is after all this time.'

The men let him go on in front, for they knew what they would do in Flosi's place.

Yet their fears were unfounded. As the farm dogs began to warn the household of strangers, Flosi came to the lighted door and stood looking at Kari, with the white snow all over his head and shoulders.

Then he came forward and, surprisingly, put his arms round Kari and said, 'I have waited for you a long while. Come inside and warm yourself by my fire. There is meat waiting to be eaten and ale to be drunk; only a fool would stay outside on a night like this. The weather gets worse and worse, the older one grows. And we are all growing old, Kari; aye, all of us.'

And when they were all seated about the feast-board, with the wicked snow rattling on the thatch, grey-haired Flosi smiled and said to Kari, 'Do you know this beautiful woman who has been sitting and smiling at you for the last hour, forgetting her meat and ale?'

Kari nodded and said, 'Yes, I know her. She is Hildigunn, your niece. I helped to kill her husband, good Hoskuld, when he went down to the cornfield for the early sowing.'

Flosi said, 'Your memory is not at fault, my friend. But it is not of early sowing we are speaking now: it is of late reaping.'

At first Kari did not understand what these words meant. But as the winter wore on, they made more and more sense to him, in Flosi's warm steading. Then, one night as they sat at meat, Flosi said gently, 'Will you marry this woman and be happy with her, and forget all the bad dreams of the past?'

Kari said, 'Yes, I will, if she will have me. I am beyond dreams now, and only see what stands before me.'

Flosi laughed and said, 'She will have you: you are now the finest man left in Iceland, as she never tires of telling us.'

Kari smiled and said, 'Oh, I don't know. There were once men like Gunnar, and Njal, and Skarp-Hedin . . .'

'Yes,' said Hildigunn, coming down the hall with her hands outstretched, 'but they have gone into the ground, and you still walk on the top.'

'Besides,' she went on, as she clasped the warrior's right hand, 'there was once a boy named Thord, and he would have grown to be a fine man. Let us pray together that God will send us another Thord, to take that boy's place and to be what the Burning never let him be.'

And so it happened. The next year they were married, and in time Kari and Hildigunn were blessed not with one son, but three: and they christened them Thord, Starkad and Flosi. Three such young hawks no chieftain ever bettered; and all that was sad in the past was forgotten in the gay cries and sunlight of the present.

As for Flosi, his end was as he would have wished, and

perhaps even as he knew it must be. When he was an old man, and happy in the family about him, he sailed over to Norway to fetch some seasoned timber for house-building, since none grew in Iceland at that time. He dawdled in Norway and enjoyed himself, bargaining and feasting. But, like many old men, he stayed too long at the board, yarning with his companions about the great days when they were all young together, and so he missed the best sailing-season; and winter, that year, came in early. Moreover, down at the quayside, wise sailors warned him that with such a load of wood on board his longship was not seaworthy.

But Flosi only laughed and said, 'Why, lads, I have sailed through worse than this in my time. And so has Kari, my dear nephew. This water we see now is like a mill-pond to that he came through, the night he landed below Svinafell. And I have no snow to go through!'

So, knowing how stubborn old men could be, the folk of Norway let him go. But they were not surprised that his ship never reached Iceland again. A viking must go his own way, even though it is under the dark water, where the great fishes hold all secrets and never tell them to any man.

Old Njal perhaps got to learn where Flosi went. Perhaps they spoke of life, together, in the end. Perhaps they even spoke of the Burning, with far-away gentle smiles, as old men do.